"SURRENDER! WE WILL NOT HARM YOU!"

Major Kira heard the man's voice call sharply from the other side of the roof.

"Do you believe him?" Lieutenant Dax asked.

In answer, Kira stood up and started firing in the direction of the voice. "Get going," she shouted at Dax. "One of us has to make it out of here!"

Dax ran across the roof to an odd, winged flying machine. Still firing, Kira watched as the birdlike machine slowly took to the air. The wind from its wings blew Kira off her feet. She hit the ground, and her phaser flew from her hand. She looked up to see the men surrounding her, weapons drawn. . . .

3/362
12

Look for STAR TREK Fiction from Pocket Books

Star Trek: The Original Series

The Ashes of Eden
Federation
Sarek
Best Destiny
Shadows on the Sun
Probe
Prime Directive
The Lost Years
Star Trek VI: The Undiscovered Country
Star Trek V: The Final Frontier
Star Trek IV: The Voyage Home
Spock's World
Enterprise
Strangers from the Sky
Final Frontier

\# 1 Star Trek: The Motion Picture
\# 2 The Entropy Effect
\# 3 The Klingon Gambit
\# 4 The Covenant of the Crown
\# 5 The Prometheus Design
\# 6 The Abode of Life
\# 7 Star Trek II: The Wrath of Khan
\# 8 Black Fire
\# 9 Triangle
\#10 Web of the Romulans
\#11 Yesterday's Son
\#12 Mutiny on the Enterprise
\#13 The Wounded Sky
\#14 The Trellisane Confrontation
\#15 Corona
\#16 The Final Reflection
\#17 Star Trek III: The Search for Spock
\#18 My Enemy, My Ally
\#19 The Tears of the Singers
\#20 The Vulcan Academy Murders
\#21 Uhura's Song
\#22 Shadow Lord
\#23 Ishmael
\#24 Killing Time
\#25 Dwellers in the Crucible
\#26 Pawns and Symbols
\#27 Mindshadow
\#28 Crisis on Centaurus
\#29 Dreadnought!
\#30 Demons

\#31 Battlestations!
\#32 Chain of Attack
\#33 Deep Domain
\#34 Dreams of the Raven
\#35 The Romulan Way
\#36 How Much for Just the Planet?
\#37 Bloodthirst
\#38 The IDIC Epidemic
\#39 Time for Yesterday
\#40 Timetrap
\#41 The Three-Minute Universe
\#42 Memory Prime
\#43 The Final Nexus
\#44 Vulcan's Glory
\#45 Double, Double
\#46 The Cry of the Onlies
\#47 The Kobayashi Maru
\#48 Rules of Engagement
\#49 The Pandora Principle
\#50 Doctor's Orders
\#51 Enemy Unseen
\#52 Home Is the Hunter
\#53 Ghost Walker
\#54 A Flag Full of Stars
\#55 Renegade
\#56 Legacy
\#57 The Rift
\#58 Faces of Fire
\#59 The Disinherited
\#60 Ice Trap
\#61 Sanctuary
\#62 Death Count
\#63 Shell Game
\#64 The Starship Trap
\#65 Windows on a Lost World
\#66 From the Depths
\#67 The Great Starship Race
\#68 Firestorm
\#69 The Patrian Transgression
\#70 Traitor Winds
\#71 Crossroad
\#72 The Better Man
\#73 Recovery
\#74 The Fearful Summons
\#75 First Frontier

Star Trek: The Next Generation

Star Trek Generations
All Good Things
Q-Squared
Dark Mirror
Descent
The Devil's Heart
Imzadi
Relics
Reunion
Unification
Metamorphosis
Vendetta
Encounter at Farpoint

1 Ghost Ship
2 The Peacekeepers
3 The Children of Hamlin
4 Survivors
5 Strike Zone
6 Power Hungry
7 Masks
8 The Captains' Honor
9 A Call to Darkness
#10 A Rock and a Hard Place
#11 Gulliver's Fugitives

#12 Doomsday World
#13 The Eyes of the Beholders
#14 Exiles
#15 Fortune's Light
#16 Contamination
#17 Boogeymen
#18 Q-in-Law
#19 Perchance to Dream
#20 Spartacus
#21 Chains of Command
#22 Imbalance
#23 War Drums
#24 Nightshade
#25 Grounded
#26 The Romulan Prize
#27 Guises of the Mind
#28 Here There Be Dragons
#29 Sins of Commission
#30 Debtors' Planet
#31 Foreign Foes
#32 Requiem
#33 Balance of Power
#34 Blaze of Glory
#35 Romulan Stratagem
#36 Into the Nebula

Star Trek: Deep Space Nine

Warped
The Search

#1 Emissary
#2 The Siege
#3 Bloodletter
#4 The Big Game
#5 Fallen Heroes

6 Betrayal
7 Warchild
8 Antimatter
9 Proud Helios
#10 Valhalla
#11 Devil in the Sky
#12 The Laertian Gamble

Star Trek: Voyager

#1 Caretaker
#2 The Escape
#3 Ragnarok
#4 Violations

STAR TREK
DEEP SPACE NINE®

THE LAERTIAN GAMBLE

Robert Sheckley

POCKET BOOKS

New York   London   Toronto   Sydney   Tokyo   Singapore

This book is a work of fiction. Names, characters, places and incidents are products of the author's imagination or are used fictitiously. Any resemblance to actual events or locales or persons, living or dead, is entirely coincidental.

An *Original* Publication of POCKET BOOKS

POCKET BOOKS, a division of Simon & Schuster Inc.
1230 Avenue of the Americas, New York, NY 10020

STAR TREK is a Registered Trademark of
Paramount Pictures.

This book is published by Pocket Books, a division of Simon & Schuster Inc., under exclusive license from Paramount Pictures.

ISBN: 0-671-88690-8

First Pocket Books printing September 1995

10 9 8 7 6 5 4 3 2 1

POCKET and colophon are registered trademarks of Simon & Schuster Inc.

Printed in the U.S.A.

To Marvin Flynn and his Twisted World

The author wishes to thank Gregor, Arnold, and the ever-helpful people at the AAA-Ace Planetary Decontamination Service.

THE LAERTIAN GAMBLE

CHAPTER
1

DR. JULIAN BASHIR was sitting alone in the little lounge just outside of Quark's Place. The lounge wasn't part of his gambling den, but Quark served drinks there anyway, and treated it like his annex. With its comfortable chairs and small tables, it provided a quiet place in the crowded space station to sit and think.

Bashir sat with a half-finished cup of coffee in front of him, playing a solitaire machine. The machine took standard Bajor coins, and Bashir had a pile of them in front of him. Julian didn't expect to win; just to pass some time. He was playing in a bored, inattentive fashion when Chief O'Brien came by.

"A good morning to you, Doctor," O'Brien said heartily.

"Is it morning?" Julian said. "How can you tell?"

"By the clocks, of course," O'Brien said. "And the station's lighting is set to a twenty-four-hour cycle to spare our old circadian rhythms—a lot of readjustment."

1

"Maybe my circadian rhythms have adjusted," Julian said. "But I haven't."

"No? I don't understand why not. You've been out here long enough."

"For what?"

"To get used to life on-station, of course."

"Maybe I've been out here long enough to get fed up."

"That would be the other possibility," O'Brien said. "What's the trouble? You look like your best girlfriend just walked out on you."

"If only that were the case," said Julian.

"What? I don't get it."

"If I had a girlfriend to walk out on me," Julian said, "at least I'd have a girlfriend. Maybe I could get her back. As it is, I don't even have a girlfriend to lose."

"What about that cute little Bajoran student you met last week?"

"You mean Leesha, the redheaded one who came through with the tour? She was very nice indeed. But she had to go back to the university. And dating is not convenient with one of us on Bajor and the other on *Deep Space Nine.*"

"You'll find another."

"But when? And how? Lately there's been a shortage of females who might be of interest to a human male."

"Of course, being a married man, I never so much as notice another woman," O'Brien said, sarcastically. "But you're not so bad off, Julian. The light of your life is still here."

Bashir nodded in understanding. "It's true. I'm crazy about Dax, but I'm finally getting it through my head that it's not reciprocated. Maybe it has something to do with her having been a man, Chief. That cramps my style."

"At least you've got your work to keep you busy."

"Recently, not even that. Everybody's been disgustingly healthy, and we haven't been visited lately by new species with interesting problems."

"Yes, it is a little quiet," O'Brien admitted. "But be thankful for it and get some rest while you can. Things always blow up again around here."

"Hah," Bashir said. "I'll believe it when I see it."

O'Brien slapped him on the shoulder and strolled off, whistling. He and Keiko, who was on an all-too-brief hiatus from her botanical research on Bajor, had just had an extremely pleasant breakfast together. At the end of it, he'd gotten a call from one of his assistants wanting him to look into an unexplained energy outage. It didn't sound like much, but O'Brien was grateful for it anyhow; it gave him something to keep him occupied.

He went into one of the elevators, and after punching the button, he thought briefly about Bashir. The doctor wasn't the sort to give up on the opposite sex for very long. No doubt someone would come along and give him a renewed interest in life. Stranger things had happened.

Bashir's mood, as he sat in the anteroom to Quark's Place, clicking two chips idly together in front of the solitaire machine, was one of self-pity aggravated by boredom.

He was wondering, not for the first time, what had possessed him to move heaven and earth to get this assignment. At the time *Deep Space Nine* had seemed the summit of his hopes and ambitions: not just the assignment to the station itself with its frontier location and its ever-changing population of races and species, but after the discovery of the nearby wormhole, access to the worlds of the Gamma Quadrant. The Bajoran wormhole was the only stable one of its kind known to the peoples of the Federation. It offered a unique opportunity to explore many worlds without being stopped by the interminable distances involved in most galactic voyages. It gave Bashir a chance to explore territory unavailable to any other human doctor, with entirely new species to look after and learn about. It even gave Bashir a chance to make a name for himself in the world of medical research.

There were drawbacks, however . . .

CHAPTER
2

THE INNER DOORS of Quark's Place opened. Out came
Quark, and beside him, but head and shoulders taller
and worlds more attractive, was a young woman. And
what a woman! She had to be a newcomer, and Dr.
Bashir hadn't even seen her come aboard. Now he
straightened up with interest.

She was tall and slender, with a great mane of tawny
hair that she kept in place with long silver pins. Her
features were delicate, but there was a look of determination about her that saved her from mere pretti-
ness. She would have been a standout anywhere; but
here on DS9 she was like a radiant young goddess. She
wore a long, pleated gown which mingled the colors of
violet and ivory. She had a tunic with built-up shoulder pads. It had frogged fastenings of gold cord, but
she had left it open in front. It was a costume Bashir
found intriguing. He wondered if it was the national
dress of some planet he didn't know about. Quark,

one hand firmly on the woman's elbow, was escorting her to the door that led out to the main concourse. And the woman, while not resisting him directly, was protesting in no uncertain terms.

Something interesting seemed to be going on. Bashir decided to deal himself in.

"What seems to be the trouble?" he asked.

"No trouble," Quark said, "the lady was just leaving."

"The lady," the woman said, "is being thrown out of this establishment by this weird-looking troglodyte."

"Thrown out?" said Bashir. "Why is the lady not acceptable in your gambling den, Quark? Are you afraid her good looks will distract your patrons?"

Bashir was rewarded by a brief flashing smile from the young lady. Quark, however, chose to take him literally.

"The people who come to my place wouldn't care who or what sat across the table from them as long as it was capable of losing money. No, it's nothing like that, Dr. Bashir. The fact is, there's nothing personal in this at all. When she came in, this lady tripped off the anti-telepath meter. It reacts to even small concentrations of psi ability in humanoids. It's a new invention from the Rhine Institute on your planet Earth. I sent for it only recently. This lady is the first one it has caught."

"Caught? That's a weighted word, Quark."

"What I mean is, the lady here tripped the alarm."

Bashir shrugged. "All right, so she's got some psi ability. So what?"

Quark sniffed and said loftily, "As I'm sure you know, nobody with telepathic or psionic abilities is allowed to gamble at my games. That's a rule observed in most gambling places. The sign is there on the wall for everyone to see."

Bashir knew the sign. It hung just inside the door, and it read, NO TELEPATHS ALLOWED WITHIN FIFTY FEET OF THE TABLES.

"I have already explained to this troll," the woman said, "that I have merely a small, latent telepathic ability of no significance. It is a telepathy shared by and limited to my species only, one that could never do me the slightest good in gambling with people of another race."

"Sounds reasonable to me," Bashir said. "What do you think, Quark?"

"I believe what the lady is saying," Quark said, with every indication of sincerity, "but it's not a matter for me to decide. 'Never gamble with a telepath' is the two hundred and sixteenth Rule of Acquisition. I have no choice in the matter. I am as bound by the rule as she is. Otherwise I'd be happy to take her word that she can't read the minds of the other players."

Quark's face took on such an expression of regret that even Julian Bashir, who knew the little Ferengi for the greedy, cynical creature that he was, was almost inclined to believe him.

"I'm afraid there's nothing anyone can do about it," Bashir said to the young woman. "And I think we can believe Quark when he tells us it isn't personal. He doesn't care whose money he takes."

"I still don't like it," the woman said. "I think it's prejudice."

"Listen, tell you what," Bashir said. "Why don't you sit down here and have a drink with me and give yourself a chance to calm down."

"Yes, why don't you?" said Quark, seeing an inexpensive way out of what could have turned into a nasty incident. "The doctor is buying and his credit is good. I'll bring them out myself. Wait till you try my Zombie Grasshoppers!" And Quark hurried off to get them.

CHAPTER
3

AS HE HAD ARRANGED, O'Brien met his assistant at the central turbolift on the forward end of the Promenade. Linc Barnoe was there waiting for him, a tall, gawky young man dressed in his best dress uniform even though he had been advised to expect dirty duty and to dress accordingly.

Linc was a graduate engineering student from Bajor University of Science and Art. He wanted to be a spacegoing engineer like O'Brien, had gotten assigned to an assistantship to O'Brien, and already he had learned more than he would have done in five years of regular practice on Bajor. He idolized O'Brien, tried to copy him in every way.

"Top of the morning to ya!" Linc said as O'Brien came up.

O'Brien nodded. He didn't like having his Irish heritage mocked, but since Linc clearly meant it as a friendly gesture, O'Brien didn't have the heart to snap at him about it. "Are those anomalies still showing up?" he asked.

"Oh, yes, sir!" Linc said. "They haven't disappeared!"

"Are you recording them?"

"Oh, yes, sir, of course!"

O'Brien had been half-expecting the traces to vanish. That was the usual fate of transient phenomena on a space station. Just when you thought you were on to something, the phenomenon faded away and the instruments dipped back to normal.

This time, however, the neutrino levels displayed on Linc's tricorder were disconcertingly high. There was also considerable activity in the photon band. So much for the tricorder analysis. Energy levels across the board were displaying a remarkable outpouring, as if a trunk line had been cut and its power diverted.

"You sure this instrument is accurate?" O'Brien asked.

"I checked it out myself only two days ago. No trouble there at all."

O'Brien studied the tricorder screen. "You got a direction for this outpouring?"

"Yes, sir. It's coming from somewhere between the second and third levels. There's fluctuation, so I can't pinpoint it exactly."

"I guess we'll have to go in and find it," O'Brien said.

"Yes, sir! Ready, sir!"

"Follow me," O'Brien said, wishing the new engineers would tone it down a little. Sometimes a simple "Okay" was better than all the "Yes, sir!"s in the world.

CHAPTER
4

QUARK WENT INSIDE, brought the drinks, and left again, smiling. Allura sipped her drink, and said, "I never thought about the telepath thing. It's always been such a minor part of my life."

"You mean you didn't know you were telepathic?"

"Of course I knew. But on Laertes where I come from, everyone is mildly telepathic, so no one's got an unfair advantage. And when we're away from home, our psi ability doesn't work on non-Laertians. So here I've come all this way to your space station, and it's cost me interstellar spaceship fares that are not refundable, to say nothing of hotel bookings that I'll have to pay for whether I use them or not. All I've gone through to get here, and now that creep of a Ferengi won't let me gamble. I mean, it's really too much." She pouted. Bashir thought she was especially fetching when she pouted.

"Yes, it is, I can see what you mean," Bashir said, thinking to himself that Allura was not only beautiful,

11

she was also spirited. He could feel himself falling in love with her already.

Bashir pulled himself up short because Allura had just asked him about himself.

Her eyes widened when he told her he was one of DS9's officers, and a medical doctor. Bashir figured she could see for herself that he was attractive and sympathetic.

Then it was her turn. She spoke of Laertes, her world on the other side of the wormhole. From what she said, Julian gathered it was an Earth-sized planet with a standard oxygen atmosphere. Beyond that, there wasn't much of interest, although the fact that it was occupied by two different but viable humanoid races was mildly interesting.

"Listen," Julian said, two drinks later, "this is such fun, why don't we go somewhere for dinner and then take in some entertainment and just keep on going?"

"That would be great fun," Allura said. "But there's something I need to do first."

"Tell me what it is. Perhaps I can help."

"Do you know the message read-out at the bottom of the main concourse?"

"Of course," Julian said. The read-out on the main concourse was a familiar feature of the ship. It was where people displayed notices for all kinds of offers to be made or received.

"Well, who do I have to see to put up a notice of my own?" Allura asked.

"I'm not quite sure," Bashir said. "I think you can access the display from almost any terminal. But why do you want to put up a notice?"

"I want to advertise for a service," she said.

"What service would that be?" Bashir asked.

"I want somebody to gamble for me," Allura said. "And I'm willing to pay."

"To gamble for you?" Bashir repeated, not sure he had quite understood.

"Since that terrible little person, Quark, won't let me gamble for myself, I'll hire someone to gamble for me. As long as this person is not a telepath, Quark can't object, can he?"

"No, I don't suppose he can," said Bashir. "Anybody with money is allowed to gamble—encouraged to, in fact.

"Good. That'll solve it."

"Will it, really?" Bashir said. "It won't be the same as you doing it yourself."

"No, but it'll be as close to that as I can get."

"True. But how could that have any interest for you?"

"I will be very interested," she said. "I believe I am a lucky person, and whoever gambles for me will have my luck. Is there anyone you can think of?"

She leaned over the table toward him. Her eyes were bottomless pools of appeal. Perfumed waves emanated from her hair. Bashir felt dizzy and intoxicated, just the way some small male spiders are said to feel just before the female devours them. Bashir had learned that in anatomy class, but he had forgotten it. It probably wouldn't have made any difference if he had remembered.

"No need to put up an ad," Bashir said grandly. "I'll be quite happy to gamble for you myself."

She stared at him, awed. "You would do that for me? You, a doctor?"

"Sure. No problem. I won't charge you anything, either."

"You are too generous!"

"Not at all," Bashir chucked. "There's something in it for me. We will be able to have dinner together, and then do whatever we want afterwards."

13

"Nothing would give me greater pleasure," Allura said. "But the gambling—it isn't quite as simple as that."

"Why not? I'll admit I'm ignorant of most games of chance, though I played a little poker in college."

"It has nothing to do with knowing a game," Allura said. "It's just that, if you're going to gamble for me as my representative, you and I must first have an agreement."

"I'd love to come to an agreement with you," Bashir said, smiling. "What sort of an agreement do you want?"

"Now, be serious! First of all, it must be understood that I will give you the money to gamble with. You will not use any of your own. Anything you lose will be from my money, and anything you win will be added to my money."

"That seems fair enough," Bashir said.

She leaned forward, lips moist, cleavage prominent. "And this next point is very important. If you're going to gamble for me, you must promise not to quit before either you or your opponent is wiped out."

"You play for blood, don't you?" Bashir said, amused.

"It is the only way to gamble. Do you want to drop out now?"

"Certainly not," Bashir said. "Please continue."

"I was saying that the game is to continue until I am broke—or until I've won everything there is to win."

"What a curious provision," Bashir said.

"I think it makes the whole thing more exciting," Allura told him. "I consider it very important."

"Yes, no doubt. Well, fine, I have no objection to this. Though I warn you, from what I know of Quark's Place, I may not last too long there, no matter how much you start me with."

14

"I'm not worried about that. I believe in my luck, and in the long-awaited luck of the Lampusan people, and in the mathematical evidence that that luck can be transferred to a proxy."

Later, Dr. Bashir was to remember that phrase she used: the long-awaited luck of the Lampusan people. And he was also to think of her phrase, "the mathematical evidence that luck can be transferred to a proxy." Right now, intent on getting on with the evening, it didn't even occur to him to ask her what she meant.

He said, "I think we've come to an agreement. Shall we get a bite to eat?"

"Yes, I'd love to," Allura said. "But first, let's get all we've said down in writing."

"In writing?" said Bashir.

"Of course," Allura said. "I believe in knowing exactly what's agreed to. But if you'd really rather not . . ."

"I don't mind at all," Bashir said grandly. "Actually, it's all rather a lark."

His cheeks were to burn later when he remembered that phrase. "Rather a lark." Hah! No lark, but rather a stinking dead vulture. But he was to think that only later. For now it was a lark, and he was embarked on a most delightful adventure after too long a time of no fun at all.

CHAPTER 5

THERE WAS A KNOCK on the door of Quark's office. "Come in," he said. The door opened and Quark's brother, Rom, popped in his head.

"I thought you'd want to know," Rom said, "that Dr. Bashir has just entered and is proposing to gamble."

Quark sat up straight. "Yes, that is interesting. Thank you, Rom. See to his needs. I'll be out presently."

Quark straightened out his clothing and came out into the gambling den that was named for him.

"Dr. Bashir! What a pleasure! But what could you possibly want here?" Quark asked. "Surely we're not going to argue any more about the woman?"

"There's nothing to argue about," Bashir said. "I've come here to gamble."

Quark looked at him suspiciously. "And what are you proposing to gamble with?"

Bashir hefted a bag that clinked as he shook it, and handed it to Quark.

Quark said, "Laertian dinars! First time I've seen them in such quantity!"

"You can have them tested if you think they're not authentic."

Quark shook his head and held a coin up to the light, then another. "They're the real goods, all right. Only the Laertians get that fine fall-off color in the blue-gray band."

Bashir took the bag back. "Laertians are new to civilized trading. How come you know about their currency already?"

"My boy, when a new currency enters the game, whether the game is interstellar commerce or gambling, all interested parties take notice very quickly indeed. A new currency is reported on quicker than a new star, and there are a lot more people interested in how it performs. Might I ask where you got this currency?"

"It's no secret," Bashir said. "Since you won't let Allura gamble herself, she has asked me to gamble for her."

"Indeed?" Quark said, with a chuckle.

"There's no objection to that, I trust?"

"None whatsoever. If you're doing it, Doctor, you can gamble as long as you wish here. As long as she is not physically present in the room with you."

"That's something else I wanted to ask you," Bashir said. "Allura has asked me to gamble as long as either she or you have any money left. Is that agreeable to you?"

Quark stared at him for a moment, then broke into a rude laugh.

"Gamble until one of us is tapped out? I couldn't

ask for anything better! As long as we play one of my house games."

"There's no problem about that," Bashir said. "I take it this Laertian currency is good?"

Quark nodded. "The L dinar, we call it. Good as latinum. Better. I won't go through all the calculations by which we decide its value in terms of gold-pressed latinum, but I'll pay you approximately 7.3442 bars per L dinar. I'll look up the exact figure later, but I think that's correct."

Bashir glanced down at a small padd, made some calculations, then nodded.

"Okay, that seems fair enough."

"So no further objections?"

"None whatsoever, Doctor. I know you're no telepath. On the contrary. You can't even read your own mind."

"Beg pardon?" Bashir said.

"Never mind. You're welcome to lose money here just the same as anyone else. I don't care whose money you play with."

"It happens to be a young woman's life savings."

"A young country's, more likely. Don't you realize how much money she gave you?"

"Help me put it into chips," said Dr. Bashir.

"Rom!" Quark called his brother, who quickly and efficiently converted Bashir's money roll into blue, red, and white chips.

CHAPTER
6

OUT IN SPACE the passenger-carrying freighter *Star of Buuler* had just emerged from the wormhole and was maneuvering into one of DS9's main docks. The *Star of Buuler,* registered at Srinagar XII, had made stops at many planets in the Gamma Quadrant, dropping off cargo and picking up passengers. After leaving its passengers, it would refuel on Bajor, and then take up its travels again.

There was a mixed lot of passengers on this trip. There were big-headed Calydonians from Lesurgis 32, small quick-talking Yentis from Alamenta II, even one Cardassian youth, taking his own personal sight-seeing trip through the galaxy and not finding much that could compare to his home planet.

And there were three Kendos from Laertes. Two of them were small, determined-looking men, dressed in baggy clothing of lavender and black that seemed the national colors of their home planet. The third, who had signed the ship's register for all three of them as

"Anatol Alleuvial and friends," was somewhat taller than the others, with light eyes and curly blond hair, and wearing rich clothing of many colors, though lavender and black predominated. He seemed to be the leader and spokesman for all of them. The others deferred to him constantly. They stayed pretty much by themselves and seemed preoccupied, not at all like typical pleasure-seekers.

There was also one Ferengi aboard, a priest in the long blue-and-yellow striped robes of his office. That was unusual; Ferengi didn't travel much, and no one had ever seen a Ferengi priest before.

CHAPTER 7

"WHAT GAME would you like to play?" Quark asked.

Bashir shrugged. "It's all the same to me."

Quark had decided to personally guide Bashir through his first evening's play, acting as his croupier, cashier, information service, and whatever else was required. Being all things to a person—that was one of Quark's best talents. It was also the essence of Kraggnish, the Ferengi art of getting your enemy to think you are his friend and dying to do him a favor, though actually you're only dying to see his latinum in your pockets. Bashir wasn't really Quark's enemy; he was almost fond of the doctor. But it was good to practice the art of Kraggnish whenever possible, just in case an opportunity came to use it.

Quark had had the gambling room redecorated recently, putting up Aneurian mood-paintings on all the walls. These were holographic illustrations of nonrepresentational objects, which morphed through a sequence of changes, accompanied by an almost undetectable low-tone musical accompaniment. The combination of the two techniques was reliably said to promote feelings of well-being and confidence in all creatures with Type B1 nervous systems. This included all humanoids, though it by no means included all sentient creatures. For some species, like the Vagrii of Solotex V, the Aneurian mood-paintings were disturbing in the extreme, and such species had to be shielded from them with Aneurian cloak baffles, which Quark provided at a nominal fee.

"You're going to have to pick one," Quark said.

"Oh, I don't know," Bashir said. "I've seen some of your patrons play a game with different colored balls that swing through the air. What's that one?"

"That's Andralor," Quark said. "I'll show you how it works."

The area where Andralor was played was decorated with alternating zebra patterns and flash squares of green, blue, and yellow. Coming up to the game position, Quark indicated a playing slot left open. Bashir stepped into it, closed the half-gate as he was directed, and put his chips into orderly stacks in front of him. With Quark's help, he lined up the ornate ivory bet holder on the brag line. Lights flashed. "It's waiting for your initial bet," said Quark.

"How much shall I wager?" Bashir asked.

Quark shrugged. "Since I represent the house, I am your opponent. Therefore I cannot advise you on the size of bets. Whatever you please."

Julian shrugged and picked up a stack of chips at random and put them on the brag line. A sigh went up from the several other players. A withered old woman gotten up like a countess in a Busby Berkeley musical muttered, "So much? And the game's high sequence just beginning?" The large, soft man beside her, a Lunarian from his pallor, said, "Do you think he knows something, or is relying on beginner's chance?"

Bashir didn't hear the countess's reply. He was too busy stacking up chips from the pile that had been pushed toward him by the orange-haired croupier who sat in the center hole of the Andralor layout dispensing the results of the action. Bashir was pleasantly surprised to find that he had won and won big. And this on his first excursion into the game.

All eyes were on him. Bashir smiled back at all the frowning faces. He pushed a stack of chips onto the brag line. "Let's play Andralor," he said. And the game proceeded.

CHAPTER
8

CHIEF O'BRIEN peered into the darkness of the inter-deck crawl area. He couldn't see a thing, but that didn't matter. Sometimes you could hear something, or even smell something—like burning insulation. But he doubted if that would account for the disturbances he was tracing.

Still . . . something had sure as heaven set off the sensors. The instruments had been registering the sudden heavy withdrawal of power from several of DS9's energy systems. The systems had been drained simultaneously as if through a thousand taps, as it were—and that was impossible, because you couldn't handle energy that way. Or could you?

At the same time, there had been unexpected photon activity, and intermittent neutrino flares. Like something was reaching into the guts of the energy stream itself and changing its composition.

Whatever it was, O'Brien had to see. It would probably turn out to be something banal and commonplace, but you could never be sure. Behind him, Linc Barnoe stirred restlessly and asked, "Want a light probe, Chief?"

"Not just yet." It was difficult to get Linc to see that you had to rely on all your senses, even when, as now, trying to trace down an energy disturbance that had come up out of nowhere and still, even as they approached its point of emanation, made no sense at all.

To make it all the worse, O'Brien didn't even know what he was looking for. Something anomalous. But by definition, what was anomalous might well not be describable or even explicable. O'Brien sniffed the wall, then played a narrow light beam across it. He commented, "Looks like it passed through here, whatever it was, the energy surge, I mean, and went up at a ninety-degree angle. I guess we'll have to go up and see what we find." He made a face.

"Go up where, sir?" Linc asked. Still new on the station, he didn't know the layout of DS9 from all angles and perspectives, as did O'Brien.

"Up to the Promenade deck. We're directly under it now. In fact, I think we're right near that new restaurant, the Bal Cabarin."

CHAPTER
9

BENJAMIN SISKO and his senior staff were at the Bal Cabarin, a smart little dinner club that had recently opened on the Promenade. It was not Sisko's sort of place at all. The idea of being entertained while dining was alien to his nature. The son of a gourmet chef, he preferred to savor his food. But this was a special occasion. The ambassador from Enten V was just leaving. He had arrived a few hours ago, first of his planet to visit DS9. Enten V was a small class-M world in the Gamma Quadrant, at the other side of the Bajoran wormhole, filled with an intelligent, hardworking species. The Entens seemed like they might make good neighbors and valuable trading partners. Hence the importance of entertaining one when he did show up at DS9.

Part of Sisko's job as commander of the station was to make gestures like this when necessary, and to do it well. He hoped he was doing it well. A glance at his two officers, Major Kira and Lieutenant Dax, gave him no special insight into how well he was doing.

The Enten ambassador, at any rate, seemed pleased enough. He wasn't really an ambassador; just the first tourist to come from Enten to DS9. But Sisko had opted to give the creature some honor, and to encourage others of his kind to come to DS9.

The ambassador looked very much like a large-headed weasel wearing spectacles. He was dressed in a richly embroidered orange kimono, and he wore various silver trinkets around his neck. These signified his rank and power among his own people.

Actually, the dinner seemed to be going very well. Sisko couldn't remember when his junior officers had been more charming. Then the first of two unusual things occurred.

Dax said to him, "Isn't that Julian over there?"

Sisko looked across the club and saw Dr. Bashir in a shadowed booth, talking with animation with a beautiful dark-haired woman whom he didn't recognize.

The second surprise was when the floor opened almost beneath Sisko's table and out from the crawlspace beneath came Chief O'Brien and one of his assistants.

CHAPTER
10

"EXCUSE ME, Commander!" It was Chief O'Brien, with his sensors and his probes, and with Linc, his assistant, trailing behind, bulling through the tea garden on the Promenade level as he looked for the source of the fluctuation. "We must have taken a wrong turn somewhere."

Sisko asked, "What are you up to, Chief?"

"It's nothing much, just tracing down a rather mysterious energy fluctuation. . . ."

"Have you got it?"

"Not yet. The trail led this way. I'll just have to see where it goes next."

"Is it anything we should be concerned about, Chief?"

O'Brien tried to formulate an answer. "It's an unknown, sir, and an unknown could potentially be just about anything. But this sort of thing usually turns out to have some perfectly simple explanation. I'll tell you about it as soon as I've got it traced out."

O'Brien and his assistant went back down into the crawlspace. When Sisko looked across the room again for Julian, he was no longer there. Too bad, Sisko thought. He liked the Doctor, and had been planning to invite him to the reception. Apparently, the Doctor had a new interest.

He returned his attention to the Enten ambassador. The ambassador was also staring across the club to where Julian and the woman had been.

"Who was that?" the ambassador asked.

"The man was my medical officer. He seems to have left before I could introduce you."

"I do not mean the man. It is the woman I refer to. The one with the young man you say is your doctor."

"Never saw her before. Why do you ask?"

"She is a Lampusan from Laertes, that's why. I recognize the look. They are planetary neighbors of ours."

"Good neighbors, I hope," Sisko said.

"Not too bad," the ambassador said, "at least unless the Lampusans get carried away with their nonsense."

That was a cryptic statement, to say the least, and Sisko would have enjoyed following up on it. But the meal was over and it was time for the Enten ambassador to depart. And there was another planetary official waiting to be greeted soon after that.

CHAPTER 11

"WELCOME BACK, DOCTOR," Quark said. A student of alien anatomy and physiognomy might have noticed that the Ferengi seemed to be distressed, though he was doing his best to appear affable. "I feared you might have reached your limit with our little game, so little did it seem to tax your skills."

"I wasn't aware of using any particular skill," Julian said. "But I was pleased to win, and I've come back to see if I could win some more."

"Just as I expected," Quark said. "I had better warn you, nobody leaves Quark's Place a permanent victor. He or she always goes back to stake their wagers again, and again, usually until all is lost."

"An unpleasant outlook, admittedly," said Julian. "But why bother to tell me about it, since my losses at the table here can only serve to enrich you?"

"I know that," Quark said, "but my long-standing friendship with you prompts me to say, don't be too reckless, for everything you've won can be wiped away in a flash."

"I guess I'll just need to see that for myself," Bashir said. "Besides, I don't care. It's not my money. May I go back to my old position at the Andralor table? I think it's lucky."

"That thought had occurred to me, too," Quark said. "I have had your seat temporarily taken out of play while my technicians examine it for signs of unfair tampering."

"Well, any chair will do," Bashir said. "What about this one here?"

Quark waved a casual hand. "Of course. Proceed, Doctor."

And Julian took out his chips and proceeded.

And once again he won.

And won.

And won some more.

CHAPTER
12

AFTER HIS SESSION at Andralor, Bashir went to the Starlight Lounge, a new place on the Promenade. Allura was waiting for him, sipping a nonalcoholic drink and looking extremely fetching.

"How did you do?" she asked.

"Rather marvelously," Bashir said. He poured his winnings on the table. He had all the L dinars she had given him earlier, plus an impressive bundle of neoflorins, ICUs, and bazmeeli. All together it made a neat little heap, and a valuable one. Quark had had to scrape the back of his safe to cash in Bashir's chips.

Allura didn't seem surprised. "That's fine, Julian. Now pick it all up again. You'll need it for the next session."

Julian said, "But I've already won a considerable amount. It more than pays your expenses from Laertes, and gives you a nice little profit as well. Are you sure you want me to go on?"

"Of course I'm sure! And you promised!"

"Oh, I'm not trying to back out," Bashir said. "Just suggesting caution. I can lose all this as fast as I won it."

"I understand that," Allura said. "But frankly, we've only begun. Why don't you have a cup of raktajino and a quick sandwich, and then go back?"

"Well, all right," Bashir said. "I had thought we might go dancing, celebrate our victory."

"Later," Allura said. "Right now, I want you to go on gambling."

"Very well," Bashir said. "I'll just order myself a little snack."

"I took the liberty of ordering something for you," Allura said. "A nice protosoy with Sweeze. Here it comes now."

A waiter came over and with a flourish put a sandwich down in front of Bashir, and a cup of coffee.

"Oh, very well," Bashir said. "You *are* eager!"

"You don't know the half of it," Allura said.

CHAPTER
13

ROM GLANCED THROUGH the peephole and said, "He's back."

"As I expected," Quark said.

Rom looked up from his pocket calculator and said, "He left here with over fifty bars of gold-pressed latinum."

"I am aware of that," Quark said. "I kept count as he played."

"He's won all the bars from the quick-cash drawer."

"I know that, too. Get some more out of the safe."

Rom looked unhappy. "No one's ever emptied the quick cash drawer before."

"Don't let it upset you," Quark said. "Beginner's luck. We'll take it all back, and more."

"Yes, brother. If you're sure . . ."

"Of course I'm sure! Do you know what the odds are against him?"

"I know that the house has a fifteen-percent advantage."

"Precisely," Quark said. "Get the money and proceed with play. The immutable law of advantage will work here as it has always done."

Rom did as he was told. Although he was Quark's brother, he had never had the fine flair for profit that Quark had. He was worried now. Never had he seen winning like Bashir had done. But if Quark thought it was all right, it had to be all right.

Quark busied himself with his ledgers. He wasn't exactly worried. But he would feel a lot better when the law of averages averaged out, as it was supposed to do.

CHAPTER
14

"HOW DO YOU THINK it went?" Sisko asked Major Kira, who was in standing beside him as he watched the departure.

"Very well indeed," Major Kira said. "You have a talent for diplomacy."

Sisko looked at her, frowning. It was not at all what he wanted to hear. It seemed to him there was something almost sleazy about being skilled at diplomacy, something that smacked of duplicity and the talents of double-dealing. Then, noting the little smile that quirked Major Kira's mouth, he realized she was kidding.

"Your day of making nice to people isn't over yet," Kira reminded him. "That bunch from Laertes is just landing. It would be good, Commander, if you welcomed them aboard station."

"I suppose," Sisko said.

"And there's also a Ferengi priest aboard."

Sisko raised an eyebrow. "That's unusual. Do I have to greet him, too?"

"I suppose you could let Quark do that," Major Kira said.

Sisko and Major Kira went to Arrivals Bay Seven, used for economy arrivals, run by jitney spaceships that worked the wormhole. The jitney ships responded whenever there was the bare minimum of passengers needed to offset the cost of fuel for the landing. It was a somewhat haphazard way to make a living, but for passengers it cost a lot less than scheduled spaceship runs.

The Kendos disembarked among the half-dozen passengers for DS9.

Sisko looked at them and thought: Ambassadors? No. Our protocol clerk must have gotten something wrong. Still, he went up to them and introduced himself.

"I am Commander Sisko. Gentlemen, welcome to DS9."

The new arrivals glanced at each other. They seemed not to have anticipated this. They were humanoids, about six feet in height, good-looking men with a coppery cast to their skins.

The foremost among them said, "It is good of you to welcome us, Captain. But please understand, we are not really ambassadors. Just citizens out on a pleasure outing. We thought we'd take a look at this station of yours."

"I am aware of that, gentlemen," Sisko said. "I am *Commander* Sisko. Permit me to wish you a pleasant stay anyhow. Someday we hope to reciprocate, come visit your planet."

"You would be most welcome there," the Kendo said. "I am called Alleuvial."

Sisko didn't catch the other names. After exchanging pleasantries, he and Major Kira watched the three stroll off toward the Promenade.

After a while, Kira said, "You know, there was something peculiar about those three."

"I thought so myself," Sisko said. "Do you have any idea what it might have been?"

"Not a clue," Major Kira said. "But they were ill at ease, and if their psychology is anything like other humanoid psychology, I'd say they had something to hide."

CHAPTER
15

SECURITY CHIEF ODO took some interest in the three Kendos shortly after Sisko welcomed them to the station. This was not long after Odo's gelatinous resting period which he had to go through once every sixteen hours before returning to the solid humanoid form he assumed to conduct his duties.

Noticing the ill-at-ease Kendos, Odo thought to himself how true it was that people bring their own mysteries to the space station. Nobody could be privy to all the twists and turns of what was going on here among the various intelligences who visited DS9. Most of the time it didn't matter. This time? Odo would have liked to know what those three had on their minds.

There was something about their walk Odo didn't like. He wondered to himself, What are those three up to? He was sure it was something. You don't hold down a job like Security Chief of DS9 as long as Odo had without from time to time getting a presentiment

of things to come. He had a sensitized nose for
trouble. He could swear that those three meant
trouble.

Almost automatically he began to follow them,
staying well behind. Then he noticed something and
his pace quickened. Allura, the Lampusan woman,
had just appeared and the three seemed to be following her.

CHAPTER
16

ALLURA HAD PLANNED to go to her room in the habitat ring. She permitted herself a smile as she considered how well things were going so far. Then she noticed the three men behind her.

They were Kendos from Laertes. Right planet, wrong people. She quickened her pace and took several side-turnings. They did likewise. Yes, they were definitely following her. And she had gotten herself into a deserted area of the station.

She wasn't sure who they were—just three males and from her own planet. They must be from the opposition. But which opposition? Within her own party or the other? And how did they get onto her so quickly? And how could she have been so silly as to get herself trapped here, in this lonely spot away from the crowds of the Promenade?

They were coming on faster and she speeded up. She needed to find her way back into crowds. But she didn't have the slightest idea where she was going.

CHAPTER
17

ALLURA RAN DOWN the long dim corridor, turned a corner, and stopped abruptly. In front of her, taking up the entire width of the corridor, was a door. It was barred, and the bars had been welded into place. A sign above it read, THIS ACCESS CLOSED UNTIL FURTHER NOTICE.

Allura turned and ran the other way, aware that her pursuers were gaining. She went through a deserted construction area—past bundles of reinforced iron bars higher than her head, various kinds of industrial equipment. Normally this area would be filled with people. But she remembered now, this was some kind of station holiday, many of the work areas were deserted. She could hear their footsteps behind her, gaining on her.

Looking ahead, she saw a place ahead where two doorways branched. This might be where she could lose them. She put on a final burst of speed, came up to the doorway . . .

And came to a stop. Two men stepped out of the doorways in front of her. The third was coming up behind. She was trapped.

All she could do now was try to brazen it out. "Hi there," she called out. "Kendos, aren't you?"

It puzzled them momentarily. "What about it?" one of the men asked.

"I'm from Laertes, too. It's true that I'm a Lampusan, but what the hell, we're all a long way from home. What say we all go somewhere and get a drink?"

They looked at her with grim amusement. "A drink? That's not our business with you at all."

"No? What is it, then?"

"You know very well. Just as we know you are Allura, a Lampusan who has presumed above your station."

They took long, black, whiplike objects from their clothing. These were Compliers, the feared razor-edged whips made from a Laertian mountain plant, which the higher castes among the Kendos had carried for centuries.

"But what is all this about?" Allura asked.

No answer until a man's deep voice from somewhere nearby said, "Yes, what *is* going on here?"

Everyone looked up. They saw a tall man in hunter-brown clothing. His partly formed face looked sharply down at them all.

CHAPTER
18

ODO SAID, "I am Security Chief Odo. I think you three had better come along with me."

The Kendos hesitated, looked Odo up and down, chatted together for a few moments in a language Odo didn't understand; then they nodded.

"We have nothing to hide," one of them, who appeared to be their leader, said in innocent tones. "And besides, there must be a misunderstanding. We have done nothing wrong."

"That's only because I showed up a little too soon," Odo said.

"Not at all! We were having a bit of a chat with the lady here. Why should we want to harm her?"

"I don't know. It's not for me to decide. But we don't allow weapons on the Promenade, so you can leave those whips with me for now. Now come along . . ."

CHAPTER
19

SISKO INTERVIEWED the Kendos with Odo standing in the back of the room, arms crossed, frowning. Their spokesman, Alleuvial, insisted it was all a misunderstanding. "May we return to the Promenade now, sir?" he asked.

"I'm afraid not," Sisko said. "You have threatened one of the visitors to this station, and have offered no explanation. I intend to hold you until I hear what you're up to."

Odo grunted approval, and said, "An excellent idea, Commander! Let me put these fellows in one of my cells. They're not much for comfort, but we supply food, water, and air. That's more than you get in some places."

He advanced on the Kendos, who shrank back against the wall.

"Commander Sisko!" cried Alleuvial. "Must we proceed in this barbaric manner?"

"It's up to you," Sisko said. "What were you trying to do to Allura?"

"Merely to frighten her, nothing more," Alleuvial said. "Would we be crazy enough to attempt murder within the hour of our arrival on your station?"

"I've heard of stranger things," Sisko said. "Why did you want to frighten Allura?"

"Commander," Alleuvial said, "I've already admitted what we came here for. If it's a crime to play a joke on a fellow planet person, then we are guilty and we await your punishment. If it is not, we will promise not to do it again, and you will be so good as to let us go."

"But I still want to know why," Sisko said.

"Unfortunately, I cannot satisfy your curiosity. It would be impossible, since it would require an understanding of the inner workings of our civilization."

"I'm willing to listen."

"But we are not willing to explain. It would take far too long."

"Whatever it was," Odo put in sarcastically, "it must have been important."

Alleuvial nodded. "It is not important only for us," he said, "but also for you. I'd keep a close watch on that woman, if I were you."

"But why?"

"Because it's important for you, here on the station," Alleuvial said, "just as it is for us down on Laertes. What that woman is doing in your gaming rooms now is liable to change the history of our planet, and of your Federation."

"Explain yourself," Sisko said.

"I'm sorry, I cannot," Alleuvial said. "I have said too much already. How can I explain Complexity Theory to you? But I thought I should give you a chance to protect yourselves."

"But against what?" Sisko asked.

Alleuvial remained stubbornly silent.

"You leave me no choice," Sisko said. "Although you are apparently guilty of no crime, your actions are suspicious in the extreme, and your refusal to offer satisfactory explanation cannot be tolerated. Odo, see that these people get back aboard the *Star of Buuler* and stay there until it departs."

"With pleasure," Odo said. "Come along."

CHAPTER
20

SISKO RETURNED to his quarters. But soon thereafter, he was called again. This time it was Dax.

"Ship coming through the wormhole, Commander."

"Must I be told about every arrival?"

"I thought you'd want to hear about this one," Dax said.

"I'll be right there," Sisko said.

When Sisko arrived in Ops, the blip on Dax's screen had grown to an icon about two inches long and growing. Dax increased the screen's magnification and studied the image.

"She looks tough," Sisko said. "That ship is possibly the most powerful weapon of war in this sector. I wonder what they want with us?"

"I think we're going to find out pretty quick," Dax said. "That superdreadnought is coming directly to our coordinates, and she's moving fast."

The ship expanded steadily. One block of stars after

another winked out on the viewscreen as the dreadnought blocked them. Observing that inexorable approach, Sisko knew a moment of apprehension. What did the ship's captain intend? Sisko considered going to red alert—though there wasn't much DS9 could do against this ship if it was on a destructive mission. Just before he could issue the order, the screen display changed.

"She's going into retrofire," Major Kira announced.

"Her screens are down," Dax said. "No sign of hostile intent, at least not at the moment."

Sisko noted that the ship had come to a full stop.

"He came pretty close," Major Kira said. "And with no preliminary announcement. This dreadnought captain has a lot to answer for."

"Perhaps he feels he commands too much power to be answerable to anyone," Sisko said. "But it's my guess we'll hear what he has to say before long."

CHAPTER 21

THE SCREEN VIEW CHANGED. They were looking into the dreadnought's busy control room. Then the image of the commander filled the screen. He was a large, serious-looking man, wearing a dark green uniform. He had close-cropped hair and flinty eyes.

He announced, "I am Soldan Nephta, commander of the *Laertes Castle,* flagship of the Laertian fleet."

Sisko was equally formal. "Commander Benjamin Sisko, in charge of this space station. Might I inquire the purpose of your visit, Captain?"

"I am here under orders. I hereby present to you Heimach Schin, fully accredited Gamemaster."

The screen view changed, showing a tall, thin man wearing a green robe with insignia attached.

A man stepped forward from the midst of the small group of nobles and ship's officers who had accompanied their commander to DS9.

CHAPTER
22

"GOOD DAY TO YOU, Commander Sisko. I am Heimach Schin, appointed Gamemaster by the Supreme Council of Laertes in charge of extra-Laertian decisions."

"Pleased to make your acquaintance," Sisko said. "How may I be of service to you?"

"I have come to adjudicate gambling disputes, Commander."

"Indeed? But we don't have any."

"I am pleased to hear that. I'll just stand by for a while in case something comes up."

Sisko was determined to be patient, even tractable, to cause no trouble. But he couldn't help feeling that something was about to go wrong. If he'd believed in such things, he would have called it a premonition.

Later he was to learn that this could be explained on the basis of Complexity Theory, whose workings frequently involved an epiphenomenon of anxieties, presentiments, surrounding new events that had just begun to take form but hadn't in fact happened yet.

Of course, Sisko didn't know about Complexity Theory yet.

But here was this Gamemaster, backed up by one hell of a strong ship of war.

"Gambling, sir," the Gamemaster told him, "is one of the highly sanctioned activities on Laertes, where it is considered tantamount to a religious duty. Those who gamble for the highest stakes are thought to be touched by the Supreme Gambler, which is our name and description of the Deity that rules us all. Although we normally leave the matter of gambling to individual conscience, sometimes a matter comes up which effects us all as a people."

"I see," Sisko said, though he didn't, at all. "And why do you come here to tell us this?"

"Because one of the subjects of our planet, a woman named Allura, is presently on your space station engaged in a gambling game for the highest stakes. Or do you deny this, Commander?"

"There's no secret about it," Sisko said. "She's here and she has come to avail herself of the gambling available on our Promenade."

"Have their been any difficulties to date between either of the gambling parties?"

Sisko assumed that the Gamemaster meant Quark as the other gambling party, Allura being the first. "No difficulty that I'm aware of."

"Excellent. Then I am here to ensure that none will take place."

CHAPTER
23

"GREETINGS TO YOU, GENTLEMEN," the Ferengi priest said. "Do you happen to know where I'd find the honorable Quark?"

The two men, tall traders from Rexion II, looked down at the Ferengi priest. One of them seemed to recognize the robes the Ferengi wore. "Are you a priest, sir?"

"Oh, indeed I am," the little Ferengi said. "Olix is my name. I belong to the order of the Charismatic Fathers of Profit and Loss."

He beamed at them. Although his features were typically Ferengi, he had none of the aura of double-dealing about him that Quark and the others on DS9 exhibited. In fact, this Ferengi in his embroidered red cloak and three-peaked headdress looked like the embodiment of innocent goodwill.

One of the traders said, "Quark can be found up there on the Promenade." He hesitated. "Father, do you know Quark personally?"

"I have not had that pleasure," Olix said. "My order has sent me out to visit the many Ferengi scattered far from their home planet and bring them the consolation of their religion."

"Quark? Religion?" the first man said, then coughed when the other poked him in the ribs.

"Straight up there on the Promenade," the second man said. "But Father—watch out for Quark. He's sharp, even for a Ferengi."

"Oh, I'll watch out for him," Olix said, "I'm pretty sharp myself."

Nodding pleasantly, the Ferengi made his way toward the Promenade.

CHAPTER
24

"OKAY, HERE GOES for a double hoop," Julian said, using game terminology he didn't fully understand, but thought sounded very tough and knowledgeable.

"You'll never hoop a double in the blue," said Quark.

"I'll get it in the blue," Julian said *"and* with a resounder prone."

"This I've got to see," Quark said.

Julian Bashir considered himself an expert now at the ancient and noble game of Andralor. And he had certainly picked up the jargon quickly. He had been having a wonderful time. Julian had not known before the thrill of ego-inflation that comes from successful gambling. Now he knew the sweet feeling of omnipotence, the godlike power that the successful gambler gets that lures him to his ruin. Only in Bashir's case, ruin was nowhere in sight.

"You'll never get a resounder prone," Quark said.

"Watch and see."

It was funny how fast the game of Andralor had come to him. A few hours ago he had barely heard of the game, and would have been hard pressed to remember even the most basic of its rules. He still didn't know what percentages favored one style of play over another. But that didn't matter. When you're a natural, odds and percentage tables don't matter. And Bashir knew he was a natural at this game. That was the only reasonable explanation, because whatever he did turned out to be a winning move.

"Here we go!"

Now he launched his ball without paying attention to where it was going, and left matter of spin to chance and happy accident. Whatever he did turned out invariably to be a winning move. And while the other players watched him with ill-concealed envy, and while Quark's morose expression turned darker and sadder as Bashir beat him time after time, Bashir simply kept on raking in the counters.

He was vaguely aware that he was winning thousands, even millions, but he didn't understand the extent of his victory until Quark suddenly put away his few remaining credit markers and said, "Sorry, Doctor, but I can't meet your bet. I regret to announce that the house is bankrupt and that the game is therefore over."

"Oh, really?" Julian said, slightly bewildered. "May I ask why?"

"Because," Quark said, his voice rising to a scream, "you have wiped me out, taken all my money, broken the bank, destroyed the pot, ruined the pitch, won!"

"Oh! I'm sorry about that," Julian said. Then he thought a moment and said, "But that's what I'm supposed to do, isn't it?"

"Yes, it is," Quark said sourly. "Never in my life have I seen such a run of luck."

"I thought I played rather well, actually," Julian said. "Well, I guess you'd better cash me in. I'll go tell Allura the news."

CHAPTER
23

CHAPTER
25

JULIAN WALKED ALONG the Promenade humming to himself. He was feeling in an excellent mood. He had won! He had done the impossible—tapped Quark out! He thought that tapped out was the right expression. It occurred to Julian that he could have made an excellent professional gambler if medicine had not claimed him instead.

What was even nicer was the fact that he had done what Allura wanted him to do, had done it successfully, and now was prepared to claim his reward. He wasn't very specific on just what his reward would be. Dinner, dancing, and who could tell what else? She would be very pleased, he was sure.

He found Allura in one of the outer lounges. She was sitting at a little table with a soft drink and a half-eaten sandwich in front of her. She had a small padd and was inputting busily when he walked up.

"Well, my dear," Bashir said. "We've won."

She looked up from her computer. "So soon?"

"It doesn't take me long, once I get going," Julian said.

"But why did you stop?"

"Quark gave up!" Julian said with a big grin. "He said he was tapped out. Do you know that expression?"

"Of course," she said. "But he couldn't be tapped out! How much did you win?"

"All this," Bashir said, and emptied his pockets. The pile of assorted bills, coins, and markers covered the little table nicely. "It's a small fortune, actually," he added.

Allura poked through the bills absentmindedly. She didn't seem pleased at all. Instead she was indignant.

"Quark can't just up and quit like that," she said. "The agreement was to continue until one or the other of us was completely bankrupt."

"That's exactly what he's claiming," Julian said.

"I don't believe it for a moment."

"But look at all the money we won!"

Allura ran her fingers carelessly through the currency. "Call that a lot? Reptile chop, that's all it is. That's probably what he keeps on hand for a day's operation."

"Sure. And that's what I won."

"But he's got more in the safe, hasn't he?"

"I suppose so," Julian said. "I don't really know."

"He has to have more! He has no right to stop the game! Isn't there a Gamemaster here?"

"I believe one arrived a little while ago," said Julian. He had noted the arrival of the super-dreadnought earlier, while he was taking a short break from the gambling.

"I must see him at once," said Allura.

"Allura, I really think . . ."

She glared at him. "Think what?"

"Well, enough's enough, isn't it?"

"You made a promise," she said, "and Quark did, too. I intend for him to keep that promise." There was a communicator on a little stand near her table. Allura picked it up. "Hello? Hello? This thing isn't working!"

"Just ask the computer to connect you," Julian suggested.

The computer was only too happy to patch her in to the Laertian ship. Soldan Nephta's square and serious face soon appeared on the tiny screen. "Yes? What is it?"

"Soldan? It is me, Allura Sagnoth."

"Sorry I didn't recognize you at first, Allura. These little screens are hell on my eyes. May I do you a service?"

"You can indeed. I need to speak to Heimach Schin immediately."

"The Gamemaster is resting. Is it anything I can help with?"

"It is a gambling dispute," Allura said.

"Ah," said Nephta. "Gambling? That's different! I'll call him immediately."

Moments later the Gamemaster appeared on the screen, rubbing sleep out of his eyes.

"A gambling dispute, you say? How lucky that I am here! I'll set up a meeting with all interested parties immediately. We'll continue in Commander Sisko's quarters."

CHAPTER
26

BASHIR, ALLURA, AND QUARK arrived almost simultaneously at Sisko's office. Bashir signalled. Allura and Quark stood nearby, not looking at each other. Sisko opened the door and stepped out into Ops, looking at them quizzically. Bashir waited for the others to speak, but they didn't, so he took the initiative.

"Captain!" Bashir said. "We have a dispute that needs to be settled."

"So the Gamemaster told me," Sisko said.

"He's here?" Allura asked.

Sisko shook his head. "He's on the screen. We've been waiting for you. Please come in."

Inside Sisko's quarters, Allura and Bashir sat together on the semicircular couch facing the big screen. Quark hesitated for a moment, then took a straight-backed chair to one side.

The Gamemaster, three times life size on the big screen, nodded. "Are all parties to the dispute present?"

"Yes, we are all here," Allura said.

Sisko asked, "What's up?"

Quark answered. "Bashir here has won everything in sight. He has broken my bank, the first time in history it has happened. I have declared him winner and closed the Andralor table. But neither he nor this lady for whom he gambles are satisfied."

"Doctor," Sisko said, "you've played and won. What seems to be the trouble?"

"I personally have no trouble," Bashir said. "It is the lady. She wants to go on."

"Even though the bank is closed?" Sisko said.

"Exactly," said Allura.

Sisko turned to her and in a kindly voice said, "You must have won a considerable fortune to break Quark's bank. Why not take your gains and go about your business?"

"That's not what I'm going to do at all," Allura said. "I came here to gamble and gamble I shall."

"But you've broken the bank!"

"I don't believe that for a minute. I know Quark says that, but I don't believe it. No professional gambler like Quark would have so little on hand that two sessions could clean him out. He just got scared of betting against my luck, though he was happy to do so when he thought I didn't have any!"

"What do you say, Quark?" Sisko asked. "Have you got any money left?"

"Of course I do," Quark said. "But so what? There's no law that says I have to wager it."

"You made an agreement!" Allura said. "You were to keep on playing until one or the other of us was really out of funds!"

"Well, that was just a manner of speaking," Quark said, with a small embarrassed laugh.

"Like hell!" Allura said. "Gamemaster, what do you say?"

"It was a solemn undertaking," the Gamemaster said. "There are witnesses to it. It seems evident to me that Quark didn't imagine it would come to this. But it has, and he's still bound."

"But if this so-called luck of hers goes on," Quark said, "she'll bankrupt me!"

"That was the agreement when we began," Allura said.

"Just a minute," Sisko said. "Let me get this straight. Are you really saying you won't stop until you bankrupt Quark?"

"He wasn't going to stop until he bankrupted *me,*" Allura said. "Fair's fair. Isn't it, Gamemaster?"

The Gamemaster, watching from the screen, nodded. "Fair's fair. Gambling agreements must be kept. That's the law of gambling."

Sisko said reasonably, "But Quark has nothing left to gamble with!"

"You are wrong about that," the Gamemaster said.

"How do you figure?" Quark asked.

"Have you no personal property?" the Gamemaster asked him.

"Of course I have personal property," Quark said. "What do you take me for, an indigent?"

"Are you not prepared to gamble it?" the Gamemaster said.

"Of course I am!" Quark said. "If Allura and Bashir are prepared to play for ancient Ferengi tapestries and my personal suite of furniture."

"It won't be necessary to play for furniture," the Gamemaster said. "I have brought people along who will be willing to convert furniture or anything else into acceptable currency. That is customary in these matters." He turned. "Alf Laffer? Are you there!"

"Indeed I am," a voice said, and then a man not much taller than Quark, but far stouter, with a rosy face and big smile, appeared on the screen. "Permission to come aboard, Commander Sisko?"

"Just one moment," Sisko said. He turned to Quark. "Are you sure you want to do this?"

"Of course I'm sure," Quark said. "This lady had a lucky run. I was prepared to let her get away with it. But if she wants to continue at my game, by my rules, I'll be happy to wipe her out once and for all."

"Okay," Sisko said. He turned to the screen. "Permission granted. Dax, beam him over."

Dax turned to the controls and was busy for a moment. The transporter glowed with energy and hummed softly. There was a glow of light, a faint hissing sound, and Alf Laffer appeared in Sisko's room.

"Now then," Laffer said, "let's see these family heirlooms of yours."

"I'll show them to you," Quark said. "But the price had better be good!"

"You'll find the price very good indeed," Laffer said. "It's money for the gambling tables, isn't it?"

"Damn right it is!"

"Then we'll be seeing it again."

Quark and Alf Laffer soon reached a generous price for Quark's so-called antiques.

With money in his pocket, Quark returned to the gambling den.

"I'm ready for you this time," he said to Bashir.

They played again. This time Quark was sure his luck had changed . . . until an hour later.

CHAPTER
27

"THAT'S IT," Quark said at last, in complete disgust. "I don't like what's going on here. You've wiped me out again. But this time I'm finished."

"Terribly sorry, old man," Bashir said.

"Oh, get out of here," Quark said.

As soon as Bashir was gone, Quark put up a sign saying CLOSED UNTIL FURTHER NOTICE. A group of Ferengi had given him the sign as a joke at a celebration some years back. Quark had never expected to use it. Ferengi businesses never close.

When Allura heard the bank was closed, she went to Quark's quarters and pounded on the door until he opened it.

She said accusingly, "You're not bankrupt!"

"No thanks to you."

"Then our agreement is to go on playing."

"No! Never! I'm through, I tell you!"

"We'll see what the Gamemaster has to say about that," Allura said.

"Quark must play on," the Gamemaster said to Sisko when the matter was referred to him.

Sisko shrugged. "It seems to me he's played long enough. He's lost all his money, and his belongings, too. What else do you expect of him?"

"Ferengi are known to have hidden resources. Let him tap some of them."

"He can if he wants to. But if he doesn't want to, neither you nor I can force him."

"On the contrary, Commander, he is bound by his terms of agreement to raise money for gambling as long as he is able. You are the master of this station. You must direct him to do whatever is necessary so that he can return to the tables."

"I can't do that," Sisko said.

"You know the ship I came on, Commander Sisko. It is a superdreadnought with full battle equipment. I have a contingent of battle-hardened Laertian Marines aboard, ready and willing to storm your station. The council of Laertes has put the ship and everyone in it under my command. If you don't make Quark continue, we will seize your station."

"I can't believe I'm hearing you correctly, Gamemaster."

"You heard me, and I stand by it."

"You have no authority to impose your will here. DS9 is not under your jurisdiction."

"That is not how we see it on Laertes," the Gamemaster said. "I am empowered by the laws of Laertes to see that fair play is done to any subject of Laertes anywhere who is engaged in gambling."

"If you attempt to board us, we will resist."

"If you resist, we will either take you over by main

force, or, if that seems too difficult, we will stand at a distance and destroy you with our main armament."

"Are you aware that we are under the general orders of the Federation Starfleet as well as the government of Bajor?" Sisko said.

The Gamemaster shrugged. "They are not here. I am here with my ship."

"And what if you kill Allura, your own subject?"

"She is free to leave, I imagine," the Gamemaster said. "If she chooses to stay, it is at her own risk."

"And you really intend to do this."

"If necessary, yes. My work is to uphold the law as it concerns gambling, not to save lives, not even the lives of my own people."

"And if you find Starfleet coming at you as a result of this?"

"That would be unfortunate for me," Heimach Schin said, "but at least I would die knowing I had done my duty."

"I'll tell Quark what you said," Sisko said. "But the decision is entirely up to him."

"He has two hours in which to make up his mind," the Gamemaster said. "After that, we take action." His image on the screen abruptly winked out.

CHAPTER
28

"ULTAB MUST HAVE visited you," Rom said, invoking the name of the ancient Ferengi deity of self-doubt.

"That's idle superstition," Quark said.

"How else do you explain your going broke?" Rom asked.

The Ferengi had never been known as an especially spiritual race. They were not like Bajorans, who had a long tradition of visions and spirituality. Ferengi didn't flaunt their religious side. But this didn't mean they didn't have one. For Ferengi, Gain was a sacred matter, and Loss was a device of the devil. The very concept of loss was inescapably tinged with the idea of supernatural retribution, which few Ferengi believed in any longer but all feared.

"If it wasn't Ultab's doing," Rom asked, "how do you explain your losing?"

That was the problem. Quark couldn't explain what had happened. He only knew it wasn't his fault. Since no Ferengi can ever admit it's his own fault if he goes broke, the reason for that occurrence—which happens as often to Ferengi as anyone else—had to be sought elsewhere. Ferengi believed in a number of evil spirits. None was feared more than Ultab, the demon of self-doubt and its dark shadow, commercial failure. When a Ferengi business went broke, his neighbors said, "Ultab must have visited him." And then they spit between their fingers. It was reverential way of saying, "Thank goodness he didn't visit me."

Going broke is a sin for a Ferengi, but it is a sin that he doesn't consider his own fault. It stands to reason that no Ferengi *wants* to go broke. So when and if he does, he must have done something wrong. Otherwise why would Ultab have visited him?

The Ferengi didn't really believe this sort of thing any longer, of course. That kind of thinking was a part of the old days of superstition. But they did fear it.

"Maybe if we made an expiatory offering," Rom said.

Quark roused himself. If in doubt, get angry, especially if it's against a brother who's dependent on you and therefore should know enough not to speak the truth.

"Rom, get out of here with your defeatist talk. I need to think."

Rom left, and Quark was sitting alone in his quarters, drinking from a bottle of Elcanian sour-mash bitter beer. He hated the taste but appreciated the effect. It was simultaneously a punishment and a way of getting drunk.

As he mused, there was a rap on the door.

"Rom," Quark said, "I told you not to bother me."

An unfamiliar voice said, "It is not Rom, my son."

"Not Rom?" Quark got up and opened the door. Outside was a Ferengi priest.

"I am Olix," the priest said. "I have come from the home planet, to bring comfort to Ferengi scattered all over the galaxy."

Quark looked him over. Olix was small even for a Ferengi. Stunted, you might say. He wore the white ruffed collar of his order—the Charismatic Fathers of Profit and Loss. Quark had heard of them. They were a variant on the mainstream of Ferengi religious thought, preaching faith in miracles of boundless profit without any real work being required.

Quark was not particularly religiously inclined, even for a Ferengi. But it was nice to see someone from the home world. And you could never get too many blessings.

"Come in, Father," Quark said.

The priest entered hesitantly, looking around with wonder at the rich appointments, the deep pile carpet, the tall red velvet curtains. The holo to one side was displaying empty space, the sort of view that Ferengi find especially restful, since there is nothing in empty space to buy and sell and the acquisitive mind can take a short rest.

"What a wonderful place you have here!" Olix said. "What a wealth of treasures you live with!"

Quark laughed cynically. "You should have seen this place yesterday, before I had to sell a lot of my better pieces."

"Sell them? Why, my son?"

Quark hadn't been planning to talk about his troubles. But something in the priest's friendly manner and meek demeanor made Quark feel that here was someone who would understand, sympathize.

"I sold them because I had to," Quark said.

"I do not understand."

"Father, you're not going to bring any comfort to me," Quark said. "I've committed the gravest sin a Ferengi can do."

"What is that, my son?"

"I've gone broke."

Olix sucked in his breath. "Through your own fault?"

For one mad moment Quark wanted to blame himself for everything. But then sanity prevailed.

"No, not my fault! I'm certainly not responsible for what has happened! I've been the victim of a plot! Forces unknown to me and beyond my control have conspired to strip me of wealth. How else could it have happened?"

Olix said, "They tell me that you run a gambling establishment, my son."

"Indeed I do, Father. Or did." Quark laughed bitterly.

"Gambling is a highly profitable enterprise, and a very spiritual one, since it performs no useful mundane work and therefore is a very pure way of acquiring wealth. Is this not so?"

"I suppose it is."

"But I understand you closed the gambling tables?"

"That's the case."

"But that's like shutting down a temple devoted to Profit! Why, my son? What terrible circumstance has turned you from the straight and narrow path of pure profit?"

Quark's answer was simplicity itself. "I have lost all my money, father."

"What has that to do with the price of rice in Jenshu Province? To use an old expression. Cannot you borrow more in the time-honored Ferengi way?"

"I suppose I could. But I choose not to, Father. It would be throwing good money after bad."

"How do you figure, my son?"

"Father, this game is rigged against me, though I don't know how."

"How could that be, my son? Are not the gambling tables yours?"

"Of course."

"And are not the odds of the game strongly in your favor?"

"Of course they are, Father. You know I wouldn't play otherwise!"

"Then what's the problem?"

"The person I'm playing against seems to be riding the most infernal wave of luck."

"Do not fall into heresy! What does luck have to do with it?"

"It's the only way I can account for my losses," Quark said. "There's got to be some factor of luck operating here that is playing hell with the house advantage and the law of averages."

"Are you saying that you no longer believe in the house advantage and the law of averages?"

"Frankly, Father, the events I've been through have shaken my faith in the eternal verities."

"Quark, my son, do not waver in your faith! Have you forgotten our ancient doctrine of Kraggnish?"

"I'll keep Kraggnish in mind, Father. But I ask you, what can I do without luck?"

The little priest answered his question with a question of his own. "What do our ancients say about luck?"

"That it is only apparent."

"Correct. And what else?"

"That it always changes."

"And what do they say about the house advantage?"

"That it is ever constant."

"And do you doubt these truths?"

"Certainly not, Father!"

"Let me ask you a direct question, then. Is your game properly rigged?"

"Do you think I've taken leave of my senses? Of course it is!"

"Then take heart, my lad, and do not let temporary losses on a properly rigged game drive you from the path of profitable virtue. Have faith in the law of averages. Take courage, put up whatever you can find to gamble with, and steal beyond that! Luck turns to whom the odds favor! That is an eternal verity. Remember what the ancient ones have promised us: The house advantage is eternal, and will win in the end!"

"I hear what you're saying, Father Olix," Quark said. "But you don't understand the situation. There's something uncanny going on here."

"I understand the eternal situation," Olix said. "Have faith in the odds and profit will be yours." He fumbled for a moment in a little purse he carried around his neck. He took something out and handed it to Quark.

"A hundred GPL bar," Quark said, unimpressed. "What am I supposed to do with this?"

"I want you to wager it for me in the game," Olix said. "It is my entire life savings. Increase it for me, my son!"

Quark just stared at him, the bar heavy in his fingers. He looked at the priest. This good man was prepared to gamble with him, to invest his own money, and without even asking for a promissory note. Quark felt the beginnings of an epiphany coming on. He stared at the priest with wonder-struck eyes.

"You want me to open the gambling again?" he whispered.

"That is up to you. I only hope you make the right decision," Olix said, and departed.

CHAPTER
29

SOMEWHERE IN FEDERATION SPACE, Allard Diceman sat in his padded control chair in Space Module 25, playing a game of computer chess and glancing out the viewport from time to time. His partner, Dane Whittier, was reclining on the acceleration couch, eating from a can of Meat Product 62, burrito-flavored soy protein, and wishing space modules had replicators. All was well, and all was quiet except for the occasional hiss as the air pressure adjusted.

With the viewport's magnification adjusted, Diceman could see the ore train that had left the Asteroids two hours ago with a full load of ore containing rare earths and metals. The ore train was made up of ninety-seven individual modules, linked together with plasteel couplings. The cab in front was maser-powered and slaved to a fixed itinerary. The ore train moved through space slowly but surely, its mirror array turning to pick up the rays of the sun, converting them to electricity and feeding them to the accumulators. Watching this was about as uneventful a job as you could ask for, required by government regulations, therefore deemed necessary, even though nothing ever happened.

Except this time.

A red light flashed on the control panel. Diceman looked up and saw that the motion indicators mounted on the radar array had picked up something. He punched the computer for a diagnostic. The computer took a few moments, then spit out its answer: MOTION DETECTED ON ORE TRAIN. INEXPLICABLE ENERGY MANIFESTATION DETECTED.

"That's strange," Diceman said, and triggered another diagnostic to trace the motion.

"What's strange?" Whittier asked.

"I'm getting indications of an energy field building around the ore train."

Whittier put down his can of burrito and slid into the control chair beside Diceman's. He pressed a repeat, read the signal, shook his head. "Instrument malfunction."

"What makes you think so?" Diceman asked.

"First of all, they use shoddy stuff. Second of all, how could there be anything going on with the maser?"

Diceman didn't like Whittier, neither his know-it-all manner nor his sharp barking voice. "I'm not so sure," he said. "There it is again."

Whittier nodded. "Yeah, I saw it. What are you going to do? Call the home office?"

Diceman shook his head. "It just calls for a notation in the log. There's no visual indication . . ."

He stopped in midsentence. Whittier stared at him. "What's the matter?"

"Did you catch the flash?"

"I wasn't looking. What are you talking about?"

"There was a violet flash. Three flashes."

"Well . . . So what?"

Diceman pointed at the viewport. Whittier looked. "Dammit, where's the ore train? You must have changed our attitude."

Diceman shook his head. "We're rock-steady." He set the monitor to 360-degree tracking. Empty space stared at him.

Whittier gaped at the screen. "Go around again!"

Diceman had already set the monitor to full tracking. He speeded up the action. Something as big as an ore train wasn't likely to be overlooked, even by high-speed tracking. He and Whittier both stared as the monitor went through three complete revolutions. The motion indicator dials were rock-steady on the gauges.

Diceman turned on the radio. "Get me company headquarters, and make it fast. We've lost an ore train!"

77

CHAPTER
30

SISKO STRETCHED OUT on his bed. This had been a very trying time, and it was a long way from over. As if matters weren't difficult enough, that fool Quark had not only lost his money, he was now losing bits and pieces of his gambling establishment. Quark losing! How could that be?

The more Sisko thought about it, the less he liked it. Something was very wrong here, but he couldn't put his finger on it. He should probably have told that Gamemaster to leave the system, back when it all began. But how could he have done that? The Gamemaster's superdreadnought outgunned DS9 by a factor of ten or perhaps a hundred to one. Or make it a thousand to one—DS9 was simply not equipped to fight a ship of war.

He had done what he had to do. Sisko had no doubt the Gamemaster wasn't bluffing when he threatened to attack DS9 if his orders were not followed. Even if there were an element of bluff, Sisko couldn't risk the consequences if he was wrong. The Laertians were going to have things their way on this gambling matter, or someone was going to pay the price.

There were innocent civilians here on the base whose lives Sisko had to think about first and foremost. His most important directive, straight from the top, was not to endanger the lives in his charge. And he was doing everything right . . .

But still, it was an irksome situation. He would be glad when Quark won back his money. Sisko was sure it would happen soon. If there was one thing Quark understood, it was money. He couldn't be wrong about this, could he? This woman, this Allura, couldn't beat the wily and experienced Quark at his own game, in his own gambling den . . . could she?

There was the sound of a buzzer. Sisko slapped on the intercom.

"Sisko here."

"Commander, this is Dax. There's a special communication for you from Captain Adams of the *Bellerophon*. Shall I pipe it down to you?"

"No, I'll come to Ops. I want to look at Adams on the big screen, see if he's got any wrinkles from his new work in Federation command."

Sisko bounced to his feet, washed his face, adjusted his uniform, and headed up to Ops. Suddenly he was feeling good. Talking to Adams usually did wonders for his moods.

Adams wasn't his usual bright and lively self. He seemed preoccupied, bothered about something. He lost no time getting right to the point.

"Ben, are any of your people on DS9 conducting unusual experiments involving the use of a lot of power?"

"No, sir, nothing like that is going on here. What seems to be the trouble?"

"We've been having some trouble in Asteroid Region G-12-P. They've been mining extensively for minerals and rare earths. They were just starting regular shipments from the region when you came to take over DS9."

"Yes, I remember."

"Well, one of the pieces of equipment they use is a maser-powered ore train. It moves slowly, but surely, and it brings huge quantities of ore to where we can get at it and process it."

"Yes, sir."

"Ben, about six hours ago, the entire maser train and its one hundred and twelve ore cars vanished."

"Vanished, sir? Do you mean they blew up?"

"I have no evidence of any explosion at or near the vicinity. All I can say for sure is, the ore train was there one moment, gone the next."

"That's very strange, sir," Sisko said.

"Just what we thought," said Adams.

"And you have no explanations?"

"We were hoping you could provide us with one."

"But how could I be involved, sir?"

"I didn't mean you personally, Ben. But what about someone or something out your way? Reason I'm asking, an energy map of the asteroid area made shortly after the anomaly occurred shows that the vanishing of the ore train was accompanied by a strangely patterned energy burst of enormous power. We don't know what it was, but we have a sequenced energy photograph of that explosion. Just before the explosion, there was a triple violet flash. Does that strike a bell?"

"Afraid not, sir."

"Our people have been able to trace the origin of that energy using initiation-indication geometry.

They traced the source of this clear across the galaxy to your vicinity."

Sisko thought at once of Chief O'Brien and his searches for anomalous electrical activity around the station. It was on the tip of his tongue to tell this to Adams; but he decided against it. He really needed some connection between the two phenomena before trying to form a connection. As it was, it was all too far-fetched to think that an unexplained electrical outburst on DS9 could have caused the disappearance of an ore train half a galaxy away.

"I'll look into it," Sisko said. "I'll let you know if I learn anything."

"Thanks, Ben. Everything going all right?"

"Yes, sir, just fine!"

CHAPTER
31

SISKO RETURNED to his quarters and busied himself with the computer. He had been spending a lot of time with it of late. First he had been checking out relevant databases and finding a lot of information about Laertes. Now he was searching for some explanation of the phenomenon Adams had told him about. The computer was indicating that it didn't have the foggiest notion. Sisko narrowed his search to the violet flashes. The computer wasn't helpful there, either. Sisko was trying to think of some other topic that might elicit the information he wanted when there was a signal at the door.

"Come in," Sisko said.

The door opened. Major Kira entered, looking worried.

"What's up?" Sisko asked.

"We've got trouble in the Replimat," Kira said.

Sisko stared at her, then laughed. It suddenly seemed funny to him that, in the midst of all his problems, Kira should come with a complaint about the Replimat.

"What's the matter?" Sisko asked. "Are the turnips overdone again?"

"This is no laughing matter," Major Kira said. "You'd better check this out yourself, Commander."

"I don't eat turnips," Sisko said. "Get O'Brien to look into it, okay?"

"This has nothing to do with turnips," Kira said. "Commander, I really think you should check this out yourself. It would take me too long to explain, and anyhow, I don't know what's going on. Not really, I mean."

"All right," Sisko said. "But this had better be good."

"It's good, all right," Kira said. "You're going to love this one."

Sisko took long angry strides down the passageway. Kira had to hurry to catch up with him. Passersby looked up in amazement as they hurried by. There were more people on the Promenade level than Sisko remembered. Ahead was a recreation area, screened off by a low wall. Sisko came around the wall, and saw there was a crowd in front of the Replimat. About a dozen of them were recently arrived contract workers from Laertes, highly noticeable in their trim suits of orange and green with black trim. They were scared but prepared to defend themselves, while the crowd was making low ominous noises and threatening gestures at them. It seemed like something was up. Sisko wanted to ask Kira about it, but now the Replimat was just a few dozen yards away.

The first thing he noticed was a couple of workmen, Laertians by the look of them, who were putting up movable barriers around the front of the Replimat.

Standing near the barriers were a dark-haired man and woman who didn't look familiar to Sisko. Standing beside them were five children ranging in age from a babe in arms all the way up to a dark-eyed girl who seemed to be about Jake's age.

"Who are those people?" Sisko whispered to Kira.

"The man's name is Nick Sardopolous," Kira whispered back. "He's the new owner of the Replimat. He and his family just recently arrived from Earth about a week ago. His daughter Zoe was in the same class as Jake before the school closed. But now his business is being expropriated by the Laertians."

"I'll speak to him later," Sisko said.

He pushed his way forward, and was stopped at the barrier by a short, plump Lampusan wearing an official-looking badge of some sort.

"No admittance, sir," the man said, civilly enough, "except for interested parties."

Sisko made himself stay calm. "Major Kira and I are very interested parties," he said.

"Then go in, by all means, sir," the Lampusan said. "We have to keep out the idle sightseers, otherwise there'd be no room for really interested parties."

"On whose orders?" Sisko asked.

"Heimach Schin, the Gamemaster. Goes without saying I wouldn't do it on my own. Not even yours truly, Alf Laffer, has the authority to do this."

"And who are you, Alf Laffer?" Sisko asked.

"The auctioneer, of course," Laffer said.

Sisko pushed into the area. There was a crowd of perhaps twenty people in the cordoned-off area in front of the Replimat. Standing in front of them, mounted on a plastic box that put him head and shoulders above the crowd, Alf Laffer was in full voice.

"This Replimat, ladies and gentlemen," he said, "is

the only low-priced eating establishment on this space station, and as such is doubly valuable. It comes fully equipped with replicators and many items of Federation technology."

A man from the crowd—a Bajoran—raised a hand, and when Laffer recognized him, asked, "How many meals a year does this Replimat serve, and what is the average asking price per meal?"

"I'm afraid I don't have that information," Laffer said. "This property has come up for sale only in the last hour. I'm offering it on an as-is basis, complete with furnishings. Who'll start the bidding at a million?"

Sisko said, "Excuse me . . ."

"Yes?" Laffer said. "Do I hear the first bid?"

"No, you do not," Sisko said. "You're making a very bad mistake. This property is not for sale."

"And how do you know that?"

"Because," Sisko said, "I am the commander of this station."

Laffer looked at him quizzically, then looked at a piece of paper in his hand. He showed it to Sisko. "Is this not correct information?"

Sisko glanced at the paper. He saw it was a sell order signed by the Gamemaster.

Sisko said, "The Gamemaster had no right to authorize you to auction off this property."

"But I do," Laffer said. "Look on the other page. One of your DS9 people has signed it."

Sisko looked, and saw Quark's large swirling signature.

"He had no right to do this!" Sisko said. "The property is not his to sell!"

"You'll have to take it up with the Gamemaster," Laffer said. "I merely sell off what I am authorized to. If the Gamemaster tells me to stop, I stop."

"I am the commander here!" Sisko said. "I order you to stop!"

"I am not under your orders," Laffer said. "Please be so kind as to take it up with Schin. Now, do I hear any bids above a million?"

Just at that moment Odo came pounding through the hallway, with three armed security officers following him closely.

"Stop at once!" Odo cried. "I don't know what this is about, but it must stop now. Get out of here, Mr. Laffer, or I'll have you dragged out."

"I am here on Heimach Schin's authority," Laffer said. "If you try to prevent me from carrying on this lawful sale, you'll have him to answer to. I'll remind you that the weaponry of our ship is trained on your station, and a platoon of Laertian Marines are armed and ready. Heimach Schin is not shy about using force."

"Let him use it," Odo responded cooly. "Get out of here at once!"

"I won't budge without orders from the Gamemaster," Laffer said. "Not if you kill me!"

Odo said, "Stand ready!" He knew the value of a good bluff.

But as Sisko observed the officers training their phasers, he realized that the Laertians did not understand bluffing. "Belay that!" he shouted.

The men hesitated, then lowered their weapons.

Odo turned to Sisko. "But, sir, these people can't be permitted—"

Sisko interrupted him. "I will handle it, Constable. Please leave things to me."

Odo looked for a moment as if he were going to argue. Then he gestured to his men and they all left.

"Thank you, sir," Laffer said once they were gone.

"That's one ill-mannered fellow you've got there, Commander!"

"With good reason," Sisko said. "Something is very wrong here. I need to talk with the Gamemaster."

"Yes, sir, you do that, sir. And I'll get on with the auction."

Ben Sisko marveled at his own self-control as he said, "Mr. Laffer, you could do both me and you a great favor."

"And what would that be, sir?"

"Postpone the auction for a while."

"But Commander! You know I can't do that! It might help you, sir, but I don't see how it would help me."

Major Kira, with a devilish gleam in her eyes, said, "Commander, why don't you explain to Mr. Laffer how it would help him?"

Sisko hadn't had time to work it out. But he heard himself saying, "Mr. Laffer, you haven't had a single bid yet."

"That's true, sir. But we're just at the beginning."

"This is a very small crowd for an important auction like this," Sisko said.

"True, sir. I was merely accommodating Quark, who wanted it done in a hurry."

"That may suit Quark," Ben said, "but it's not in your own best interests. Why not give it a few days, pass the word around to interested parties, give them time to get here, and then hold a *real* auction?"

"But I've already advanced money to Quark against this sale," Laffer protested.

"What of it? You'll get it back and plenty more besides. You work on commission, don't you?"

Laffer nodded.

"Then just think how much more you and your

backers are going to get by waiting. Why, I might even bid on the property myself."

"Really, sir?"

"Of course. I've always wanted a Replimat."

"Well, that puts a different complexion on it," Laffer said. "You taking a personal interest in this, I mean. I'm glad to see you're a reasonable man to deal with, Commander. I'll postpone the auction for a while, until I can get a decent-sized crowd here. And I'll make sure you're notified beforehand when I begin the auction again, sir!"

"That's good of you," Sisko said. "Come on, Kira, we have work to do."

They walked off together down the corridor, Sisko walking fast and Kira hurrying to keep up with him.

"Where is our reasonable commander going in such a rush?" she asked.

"To Ops. I need to talk with the Gamemaster at once. And then with Quark. And then we'll see how reasonable I am!"

Before he could leave, however, a medium-sized tubby man with curly black hair and tragic dark eyes grabbed Sisko by the sleeve. Sisko pulled himself free and learned that this was Nicolas Sardopolous, the owner of the Replimat. The man was heartbroken. His Replimat, bought with his parents' savings from a lifetime of selling grape leaves in Adrianopolis in Macedonia, his Replimat, which was to support not only himself, his parents, and his wife and four children, but also several cousins, was being taken away by aliens. And people were telling him there was nothing he could do.

Sisko said, "Mr. Sardopolous, please pull yourself together. This isn't your personal loss. Whatever loss is involved—and there many be no loss at all when everything is straightened out—will be handled by the Federation."

"It will, sir? I won't lose everything?"

"You have my personal guarantee that you won't lose by this," Sisko said.

"Wow!" Sardopolous was stunned for a moment. Then he said, "Thanks a lot, Commander!"

"You might have come to my office and asked me," Sisko said, "instead of planning this demonstration."

Sardopolous muttered, "Where I come from, we demonstrate first, think later. But no more demonstration. It will be as you want it, Commander."

"Good. Now, another thing. You know that section where the Promenade is being repaired on C deck?"

"Yes, of course, sir. Why?"

"What I suggest you do is put up a tent there. We'll round up a work crew to move your equipment. You're going back into business, Sardopolous!"

"I am, sir? But how can that be? I have no right to that new piece of the Promenade."

"I'm saying you do," Sisko said. "It'll be yours until we can clear up this mess and get your stuff back and your Replimat working again."

"Commander, I just want to be back in business, feeding my people! Thank you, sir!"

And Sardopolous dashed off looking for a bunch of guys to help him set up. "Everybody! Help me out! I'm opening tonight! My dinner tonight will be on the house! Pasticchio and Greek salad, finest cuisine of Mother Earth!"

People cheered. A work party was soon formed.

From behind Sisko, Chief O'Brien stepped forward. "You handled that one nicely, sir," O'Brien said.

"Thanks, Chief. But if this goes on, I don't know how we'll do with the next."

"You'll think of something, sir."

"I hope so. What are you going to do?"

"I have to see Dr. Bashir for a moment," O'Brien said. "After that, I'll see."

"Good enough, Chief." And Sisko went off wearily to his quarters.

CHAPTER
32

THE GAMEMASTER'S FACE came up on the screen. "Yes, Commander. What can I do for you?"

"I want to know," Sisko said, "if you did indeed buy the Replimat from Quark, or has all this some ridiculous mistake?"

"It's certainly no mistake," the Gamemaster replied. "After he had exhausted his own personal property, Mr. Quark asked if there was any way he could go on. I told him that as one of the original settlers on DS9, he could be considered a part-owner of the station."

"Quark, an owner of the station? That's impossible!"

"Not at all, Commander. Laertian law stipulates that those occupying a premises are to be considered joint owners of it, and are free to wager all or part of it, and to sell their share of it if necessary to satisfy gambling debts."

"The ownership of this station has nothing to do with Quark!"

"Indeed? Do you have papers specifically excluding him from participation?"

"No, of course not. There's never been any need for such a document."

"I'm afraid there is, under Laertian law."

"I tell you, he can't do that!"

"He can, and has. He really had no other option, Commander. The terms of the game were that both parties would play until one was no longer financially able to continue. If Quark had not pledged the Replimat, we would have been compelled to seize your entire station."

"That would have been illegal in terms of both Bajoran and Federation law."

"But not in terms of Laertian law. And that is the law I follow."

"You haven't heard the end of this," Sisko said. "I'll get back to you. First I have to talk with Quark."

CHAPTER
33

SISKO FOUND QUARK in his bar, making a complex combination bet against Bashir. There was a small crowd of hushed and interested spectators watching. No one else was playing, only Quark and Bashir, head on head.

When Sisko came in, Quark said, "Could it wait until later, Commander? I'm dealing with quite a complex situation at the moment."

Sisko was amazed at the Ferengi's sang-froid. "You think you've got a situation now? Talk to me immediately or I'll show you what difficult really is."

"Oh, very well," Quark said. "Let's step into my office."

Quark turned his bets over to Rom, then led Sisko to his apartment. Once inside he said, "Can I pour you a drink, Commander? On me, of course."

"All I want from you," Sisko said, "is an explanation. Did you really put up the Replimat and then lose it?"

"Yes, I did," Quark said, "But I did it for all of us."

"Now I've heard everything," Sisko said.

"But it's true!" Quark said. "I'm amazed you can't appreciate it. It's one of the few selfless things I've done in my life!"

"You call selling our Replimat a selfless act?"

"The Gamemaster was going to seize the property anyway. He's ruled that I'm a part-owner here, and that as long as I have anything to sell, I must under the terms of the agreement go on gambling."

"If you'd waited and consulted me first," Sisko said, "at least we'd have a legal case against him. By agreeing with his interpretation of the law, you've put us into a very bad situation."

"I thought about consulting you," Quark said, "but I decided you wouldn't go for it."

"You're right about that."

"Let me get you a drink, Commander, and I'll explain."

"I don't want a drink. But do want an explanation."

Quark poured himself two inches of Senlis, the powerful greenish-yellow liqueur from Carioca II. He threw it down, coughed, and sat down on a chair facing Sisko.

"Commander Sisko, this is the biggest break of our lives. We're all partners in this, and we're all going to get rich! I've drawn up a paper to state this. I've got it right here. When we break Allura, we'll be rich beyond the wildest dreams of avarice. Don't you understand, Commander, she is bound by her own rules! She has to continue just like I do, spending her money and borrowing more, until we break her."

"That's great," Sisko said. "But so far, she's doing all the winning."

"That's the delicious part. Her wins have lulled her into a false sense of security."

"I see nothing false about it," Sisko said.

"It has to be false! The house advantage always wins in the end. We just have to stick it out until the odds, the immutable odds, turn in your favor."

"And what if she outlasts us?"

"Impossible!" Quark said. "She's only one woman."

"I'm beginning to suspect she has backers."

"The more the merrier. We'll take all their money."

"I've done a little checking," Sisko said. "It's possible that she has the resources of the entire Lampusan people behind her."

"How many is that?" Quark asked.

"One or two hundred million. And if the Lampusans win this election, they'll have the entire resources of their planet to throw into this game."

"You're too pessimistic, Commander. We'll last her out. She's going to break."

"But when?"

"I don't know exactly,"

"Will it be before you sell off the rest of the station?"

"Commander, that's unkind! This is going to work out to all our advantage. And anyhow, at this point there's nothing else we can do. What I don't gamble, Schin will simply appropriate."

Sisko said, "Nothing else? We'll see about that." He stalked out of Quark's quarters and slapped the communicator on his chest. "Kira, Dax, I want to see you both immediately in my quarters. Odo, you too."

He walked out of Quark's office and saw Bashir, a silly smile on his face, waiting to wager again.

"Bashir, I need to talk to you, too. Now."

CHAPTER
34

THERE IS A CERTAIN LOOK that men get when their every
move turns out to be absolutely correct and right on.
It is difficult to characterize that look, since great and
continued good luck comes up so seldom in the lives
of most humanoids. Whatever you called it, Dr.
Julian Bashir was wearing that expression now. He
seemed so pleased with himself that Sisko, who had
sent for him, could have kicked him out of his room
with great alacrity, if only he did not need a favor
from Bashir.

"So . . ." Sisko said. "Going well, is it?"

"Unbelievably well," Bashir said. "I really think I
must be some kind of a natural at this gambling stuff.
I just seem to have natural flare. It's the only way to
account for all my winning."

"The winning is what I want to talk to you about,"
Sisko said.

"Yes, sir," Julian said. "I suppose it's been rather
hard on Quark, sir."

"It has. But that's my concern. Your concern, Dr. Bashir, is this: I'm afraid that your victories are jeopardizing our status on DS9."

"Sir?"

"Didn't you know any of this?"

"No sir. I've been . . . occupied."

"We've been visited by a Gamemaster from Laertes. He came in a superdreadnought."

"Why?"

"Because he's going to blow us apart or take us over if things don't go according to his rules."

"What rules are those, sir?"

"Quark has to continue playing as long as he can. The Gamemaster has ruled that Quark can pledge pieces of the station to match your bets."

"But sir," Julian said, puzzled. "He can't do that. The station isn't Quark's property."

"Exactly what I pointed out. But I was overruled. The station is being gambled away beneath our feet."

"Why, that's shocking," Julian said. "I had no idea Allura and her people had gone that far."

"I'm afraid the lady has been quite unscrupulous," Sisko said.

"I wish I hadn't given my promise to continue playing as long as either side had any money," Bashir said. "But what you've just told me changes things. I'll go to the Gamemaster at once and tell him I'm quitting. We'll put an end to this whole thing at once."

"That will be fine," Sisko said. "I just hope he lets you do it."

"I'd like to see him try to stop me!" Julian said.

"Let's see what conditions he sets," Sisko said. "Let me know immediately, all right?"

Bashir saluted and hurried out of the stateroom.

CHAPTER
35

"FRANKLY," SISKO SAID, "I blame myself."

Dax and Kira were in his quarters, where Sisko had summoned them.

"I don't see how you can say that, Commander," Kira said.

"I was thinking of the many emergencies I've been through in the course of my years. It seems as if, when you've been through as much as I have, you'd have a way of foretelling in advance what was going to happen. You'd think you'd have second sight, know something was wrong before it had even begun. I should have known that Bashir wouldn't stay away from someone who looked like Allura. But frankly, she didn't appear to be a harmful influence. And no one begrudges the Doctor's desire for companionship."

"And the way he's been pining lately, we all hoped this was the woman of his dreams," Kira said. "He's been looking for a long time for someone he could get dramatic with. And now, I'm afraid he's found her. But there was no way to predict the results."

Dax said, "I don't believe I had any ominous premonitions either. Did you, Commander?"

"As a matter of fact, I did," Sisko said. "But then, I usually expect the worst. My son has pointed out that tendency to me from time to time." And before that, his wife, he thought.

"Well, I didn't expect it," Dax said. "But maybe it's good it came up as suddenly as it did. At least we'll take care of it and move on to something else."

"You think we can control it?" Sisko asked.

"We're all still functioning," Dax pointed out.

"What I'd like to know," Sisko said, "is how Allura keeps on winning all the time."

Dax nodded. "That's the place to begin. I think we're stymied until we know."

Sisko nodded. "We know very little about Laertes. What little I've learned points to a complex civilization, and a great struggle between two races."

Dax said, "I feel the events here on DS9 are connected with events on Laertes in some way we don't understand."

Just then O'Brien signalled and entered.

"What's up, Chief?" Sisko asked.

O'Brien looked satisfied with himself. There was a smudge of grease on the end of his nose from crawling around the dark passageways within the station. Linc, his assistant, wasn't with him. O'Brien had sent him to get some dinner and a few hours' sleep while he reported to Sisko.

"It's that anomaly. I've got it tracked. I know its time and duration of occurrence."

"Yes? What's the point?"

"The point is," O'Brien said, "near as I can make out, the anomaly started the moment Allura came on the station, and gets worse every time Julian places a bet."

"Now what in thunderation could that mean?" Sisko asked.

"I don't know, sir," O'Brien said.

Sisko pondered for a while. "Could the linkage be accidental?"

"I don't think so, Commander. I've noted it several times."

"Are you trying to tell me that Julian is doing this?"

"No, sir. I think that whatever is causing this comes from the woman, from Allura, sir. She's never far from Quark's when the anomaly occurs. And the problems started when she arrived."

Sisko shook his head. "That's not enough, Chief. I need answers, not another mystery."

"I know. I'm sorry, sir."

"Whatever it is," Dax said, "the solution is going to be on Laertes."

"I've pretty much come to that conclusion myself," Sisko said. "We need to learn what sort of place Laertes is, what's going on there that might account for Allura's luck, and how this ties into the anomalies."

"I agree, sir," Kira said.

"That's what I want you and Major Kira to find out," Sisko said.

"You mean you want us to check out the situation on Laertes?"

"Exactly."

"Nothing I'd like better, Benjamin," Dax said.

"Remember, I'll be expecting you to find something out, not go sightseeing," Sisko warned.

"It could come down to the same thing," Kira said. "We don't even know what we'll be looking for. Our best strategy is to see what we find."

Sisko frowned. "You might want to look up that Laertian, Alleuvial. I'm sure we have his full name and address in the log. He was hinting at something but I don't know what." Sisko considered for a moment then said, "I should have let him frighten her, or whatever he was trying to do."

Dax said, "Relax, Benjamin, we'll sort this thing out if it's at all possible. We don't know what we're looking for so we'll have to hope for luck to help us find it."

"Whatever we're looking for," Sisko said, "I just hope you can find it soon."

CHAPTER
36

ODO DIDN'T LIKE going on his usual rounds, because nowadays he couldn't tell how anything should be. Just hours ago he had spotted a small Dalmatiano, a being from Dalmas II, staggering along under the weight of a big parcel. The parcel was wrapped with transparent wrapping paper, and Odo could see inside it the African masks that belonged to Commander Sisko. He didn't know where Sisko had gotten them, but they were rare and old and valuable, the only valuable things Sisko had, to the best of Odo's knowledge. Odo wasn't going to stand around and watch some thief take them away. "Stop, thief!" he cried, and hastened in pursuit.

The Dalmatiano stopped at the first outcry. He waited while Odo loped up to him. Then he said, "Is something the matter, Constable?"

"You'd better believe it," Odo said. "What are you doing walking off with the commander's possessions?"

"I'm taking it to an auctioneer, to get it appraised. Then I'll ship it back home to Dalmas. I have a curio shop in the city of Urgine. We always can use rare and unusual items like this."

"No doubt," Odo said. "But you can't go stealing ours. Please put down those objects immediately."

"Stealing? You accuse me of stealing? My good fellow, I can have you brought up on charges for that."

"I suppose the commander just handed these things over to you?" Odo asked.

"Not at all. Sisko must have given them to Quark, because the Gamemaster advanced Quark money against them, gold-pressed bars of latinum, the very best currency there is. And Quark lost again to the divine Allura and her consort, the young Dr. Bashir."

"Divinely lucky, I'll give her that," Odo said. "Let's see your bill of sale. Or don't you have one?"

"Of course I have one," the Dalmatiano said, and reached into his stomach pouch, "Here it is."

Odo read it over. Its form was unimpeachable, even to his practiced eye. Odo handed it back, turned on his heel, and left.

"Next time think again before you call a perfectly respectable Dalmatiano a thief!" the Dalmatiano called out behind him.

Odo ground his teeth and kept on walking.

He was on the habitat ring, and he continued walking past the quarters. All of the available space was taken up now. People had come from far and wide, because news of what was happening on DS9 seemed to move with the speed of light. There were Dirsinians from Ambrose's Star, little fellows who economized on rent by sleeping twelve to a room. There were the big Grumblers from the manufacturing satellites in the vicinity of Barnard's Star. They needed an entire cabin each, and even that barely sufficed. The other interested parties, creatures more similar in size to humanoids, were doubling or tripling up in the rooms.

Odo was on his way to the his office.

Intent on his thoughts, Odo opened the door to his office. But before he could go in, a rattling sound down the corridor caught his attention. He looked up, heard the sound repeated, and went to investigate.

Yes, just as he had suspected, someone was trying to get into a security panel. It was a humanoid, and he had brought a laser cutter and a wrench, and was nearly through the lock when Odo came silently up behind him and rested a hand on his shoulder.

"And what do you think you're doing?"

It was a Lampusan from Laertes whom he had interrupted, and the man looked up with a defiant air.

"I'm trying to get into the security panel, what does it look like I'm trying to do?"

Odo held in his temper. "And what do you want from the security panel?"

"Weapons access, of course."

"No weapons are allowed here," Odo said.

"I was going to seal them and take them out to my space launch," the Lampusan said.

"You have a bill of sale, I suppose?"

"I've got the owner's permission." He showed Odo a message padd.

Odo read it. "This says that all hand weapons are assigned to you for value received as soon as they are in the custody of the Gamemaster."

"That is correct."

"But you don't have a paper saying that these weapons are in fact the property of the Gamemaster."

"My dear sir," said the Lampusan, "that is a stupid

delaying tactic. These weapons have been pledged against money for this afternoon's play."

"Quark's doing, I suppose?"

"Of course. Quark is gambling on behalf of the station, I believe."

"Get out of here," Odo said in a low voice.

"What are you saying?"

"I'm telling you to get away from this area at once. Your documents are not in order. And even if they were, I would not give you the station's weapons."

"If you don't want to give them," the Lampusan said, "you shouldn't have pledged them in the game."

"I didn't pledge them," Odo said. "Someone else did, but he had no right to." Odo sighed. "Let me make it clearer," he said. "You Lampusans have gone far enough. This whole thing, the Gamemaster and all of it, is just a license for you people to steal. Do you think your ship out there means anything to me? I'm interested in what is right, and this is not right."

"Others have agreed to this," the Lampusan said. "You had better, too."

"I'm giving you ten seconds to get out of here," Odo said. "Then I'm going to come after you and take you away by the scruff of your neck. One, two . . ."

He didn't have to go past five. The Lampusan was gone, swearing he'd return.

"Fine," Odo said. "I'll be ready for you." This nonsense had gone on long enough.

CHAPTER
37

SCHIN THE GAMEMASTER arrived at DS9 in his own launch, accompanied by a guard of honor. The Gamemaster was affable, and Sisko showed him around the station and then assigned him a temporary office.

Sisko was just leaving when Julian Bashir appeared and requested an interview with the Gamemaster. Schin granted it. Sisko left them and returned to his own quarters.

Sisko lay down on the couch to get a moment's sleep.

Not ten minutes later there was a signal at the door. "Come in!" Sisko called out. The door opened. In came Bashir.

"What happened?" Sisko asked.

"I told the Gamemaster I wanted to stop gambling. He read me the riot act," Bashir said. "He said I had made an agreement to continue gambling except given certain conditions, namely, the absolute bankrupting of either Allura or Quark. Since these conditions hadn't been met, I was morally and legally bound to continue. He said I could quit, of course, but in that case Allura would be permitted to gamble in her own right, or to nominate someone else. And if for any reason Allura or a substitute was unable to continue, the station and its contents were forfeit to the Lampusan People's Party, her sponsor. In short, Commander, there's no stopping what's going on by me stopping gambling. I thought it would be less complicated if I continued. At least that way I can keep an eye on them."

"You did right," Sisko said. "Kira and Dax have volunteered to go to Laertes and see if they can figure out what's going on there and what it has to do with here."

"I wish I could come, too," Bashir said. "But I guess I'm needed here to go on with the gambling. Weird situation, eh, Commander?"

Bashir left Sisko's room and took a turbolift back to the Promenade level and the game.

CHAPTER 38

DAX WAS SITTING in a small shop on the Promenade deck, sipping a double Quadrian mocha and reading a science journal on a table screen. She looked up when Quark came in.

"Hello! Thanks for making time for me!"

"No trouble at all," Quark said sourly. "I have nothing to do these days but lose money to Dr. Bashir. That's so simple that I can turn it over to one of my assistants. I don't need to be around to witness the total collapse of all my enterprises. What do you think of that?"

"I think you're feeling very sorry for yourself," Dax said.

Quark looked surprised. "But of course I am! When something goes wrong with a Ferengi, he's *supposed* to feel sorry for himself, and complain about it as loud and as often as he can! Otherwise he would be considered lacking in self-respect!"

"No one would ever accuse you of that," Dax said.

"I'm happy to hear it," Quark said, ignoring the irony in her voice. "I must get back soon and lose some more. What did you want to see me about?"

"I want to ask your advice."

Quark looked surprised. "On what? The art of losing?"

Dax shook her head. "If there's one thing you know about, it's the psychology of gambling."

"It doesn't look like I know much now, losing as badly as I am."

"I don't believe that, Quark. I know it's not going well for you at present. But I suspect you're up against something that was set up. I think that in one way or another means somebody's taking advantage of you."

"I'm being cheated!" Quark said. "I suspected it!"

Dax shook her head. "I don't necessarily mean cheating. But something is happening here that has little or nothing to do with gambling or the odds on one number or another coming up."

"You're right about that," Quark said. "Something very odd is going on. You're going to have to find out what it is."

"That's what I intend to do. But first, give me a snap judgment on this—is Allura a winner or a loser?"

Quark grimaced and said, "She's beating the hell out of me at present. But I'm betting that Allura is a loser in the long run, no matter how much she wins in the short run. Don't ask me why. It's just a feeling."

"Do you think her victory over you has anything to do with Bashir?"

Quark shook his head. "I don't think the good doctor counts for anything in this game. He's just there to push the markers. From what I've heard, this is really a contest between DS9 and the Lampusans of

Laertes. Bashir is just riding on Allura's luck. Or maybe he's an extension of it."

"But despite that, you still think Allura's a loser?"

"Yes. What little I've learned about the history of her people, the Lampusans of Laertes, seems to bear me out. She's a loser from a race of losers. But right now she's winning like crazy and I may go broke before I get a chance to prove that."

"Thanks," Dax said. "That confirms my own suspicions. I've got to go now, Quark. Thanks for your advice."

"I only hope you can use it to do me some good," Quark said.

CHAPTER
39

THE *LUCKY STAR*, a freelance luxury cruiser licensed to the Altuna group, was at Docking Pylon F, pocked silver skin glistening against the stars. This was the outermost section of the docking ring, wherein could be found the docking ports and cargo bays. To one side were the facilities for the mining operations that had been *Deep Space Nine*'s first order of business under the Cardassians. Beyond that were six protruding docking pylons. Small tractors moved back and forth beneath its curving hull, delivering last-minute supplies. The purser was standing by the airlock in a dress uniform, checking off passengers' names on a clipboard and talking to the bridge on a communicator. The last passengers were just coming aboard. Departure was minutes away.

Kira and Dax came through the airlock at the last moment. "I hate this," Kira said. "If the Lampusans had left us even *one* runabout . . ." As they reached the gangplank, a crane swung nearby with a slingful of goods and furniture bound for Laertes. The two women stared at it.

"Hey, isn't that my couch in there?" Dax asked.

"Yes, and my dresser!" said Kira. "How did Quark have the nerve to gamble it? How dare he spend other's people money on gambling?"

"Quark never has a problem spending other people's money," Kira said.

A steward led them belowdecks and showed them their accommodations. They had booked a cabin despite the short duration of the trip via wormhole. Their room was small but fully equipped. It had two bunk beds, dressers built into the wall, even a small private bathroom with sink, commode, and bidet. The walls here were a simulated wood design. Indirect lights were set into the walls.

They unpacked, leaving the door into the corridor open because it was too crowded in their little room otherwise.

Then the *Lucky Star*'s klaxon sounded and the vibration of the ship's impellers increased, and moments later the ship was on its way. They went to the observation deck. Here they saw the great swirling purple lines of the wormhole, with a violet nimbus playing between them, and then they were in it.

Once the journey was under way, Dax and Kira went for a stroll. The *Lucky Star* was a fairly new ship, equipped with four restaurants and three swimming pools. Dax decided there was enough time for a dip before dinner. Kira joined her. They had been long enough on DS9 to appreciate an Olympic-sized pool.

The swimming pool was equipped with individually focusing heating and tanning units set in the ceiling. You could dial up any degree of tan you desired. The two enjoyed the water, but declined the tanning, which they considered barbaric.

That night they ate at the captain's table. He appeared to be a gallant officer, a Kendo, with all the good luck and powerful charm of that people. His name was Spiq.

"I hope everything has been to your liking thus far?"

"It has all been fine," Kira said, for it was she whom Spiq addressed. "I've noticed, however, that most of the ship's crew seem to be Kendos. I mean no offense by pointing this out."

"None taken," the captain said. "It is self-evident anyway. The explanation, dear lady, is simple. Our worthy second race of the planet Laertes, the Lampusans, usually prefers to stay home, not go out to meet strangers from the far corners of the galaxies."

"Interesting," Kira said. The captain smiled and went back to his guests. Soon a waiter came by and the women ordered a good dinner from the well-stocked *Lucky Star* menu.

They went for a stroll after dinner, through dioramas showing sights that they would be able to see on Laertes. The Boiling Gardens of Landisfree looked interesting, as did the Speeding Rocks of the Bacl Glades.

There was just time for one more swim in the pool. Then the warning klaxon sounded. Laertes was dead ahead. And soon they saw it on the ship's main screen, a big green and purple planet.

Meanwhile, elsewhere in the universe, anomalies were on the increase. In unauthorized fleet maneuvers held by the Chronitic people of Althon IV, the midship of three vanished suddenly and unaccountably, resulting in the loss of seventy-eight lives. The Chronitic people blamed this on the Federation and entered suit in high court.

On Alman XII, a small, barren world circling a fading red dwarf, nearly a third of a solar observatory vanished. Luckily, no people were injured. The anomaly continued to creep, forcing evacuation of the nearby industrial park, which had been devoted to high-vacuum automatic engineering.

On Celsus II, in the region known as the Great Nothing, a jagged ravine twenty miles in average diameter and extending for almost a thousand miles was carved into the skin of the planet. No lives were lost. Bizarrely enough, this accidental excavation revealed huge deposits of useful ores. The owners pressed to have the anomaly studied but "not corrected until its economic uses could be ascertained."

Matters didn't turn out so well for the *Melbourne Queen,* a superliner carrying nearly two hundred passengers. The anomaly sheared off the rear third of the ship as cleanly as though done with tin snips. Automatic doors closed in time to preserve the internal atmosphere through the rest of the ship. Curiously, no passengers or humans of any sort were lost, but a herd of prize Herefords bound for Ouna IV vanished into the anomaly.

CHAPTER
40

"RIGHT OVER HERE, LADIES! Your baggage!"

There was a good-sized crowd getting off at Laertes. Klingons, Braswells and a delegation of Trollites from Dexus II, looking to sell the rare earth mixtures that the volcanic action on their planet produced. Events of the last two years had put this planet on the Gamma Quadrant map. Trade and travel, those concomitants of civilization, were already well established.

Kira and Dax came down the gangplank onto the landing stage. Entrance formalities were simple. With a quick glance at their credentials, the purser waved them through.

"What city is this?" Kira asked.

The purser smiled. "This is Sgheel, ladies, Laertes' capital city. A fair and smiling place, replete with all civilized amenities. Everybody likes this place."

Kira and Dax left the landing stage and walked into

the crowd that had gathered to witness the ship's arrival. A child, standing at the foot of the gangplank, rushed up with a big basket of flowers. Quickly she made a selection and gave both officers garlands of white ote blossoms.

CHAPTER
41

THEY CONCLUDED THEIR WALK that first day by going to an outdoor terrace cafe set high on the heights of Banneria, with a fine view of the city below and the plain of the Scarmodes beyond. They sat and looked over the steep-pitched roofs of the city. Soon the waiter came over. Even even though he hadn't yet taken their order, he was carrying two drinks.

"What's this?" Kira asked.

"Your drinks."

"But we didn't order anything yet."

"I know. I took the liberty of intuiting your preferences in the way of drinks. I can always take them back if you'd prefer something else."

The drinks—a Martian Sunset for Kira and a Black Hole for Dax—were perfect, and just what they had been planning to order.

"How did you know what to bring us?" Dax asked.

The waiter shrugged. "We Laertians always anticipate. It's just how things work on Laertes."

After leaving the cafe, they found a pleasant little gift shop. It was packed from wall to wall with a dismaying assortment of goods—souvenirs of all sorts, commemorative cups, gold bowling balls with microscopic engraving on them, crystals with snowflakes frozen inside of them, drops of water encased in crystal and taken from famous Springs of Langeshaven, and many other things. Seeing all this, Dax thought of something she'd like to buy, but she couldn't remember what it was called.

Unperturbed, a salesclerk came over quickly and said, "Oh, I think I know what you mean," and produced in a matter of seconds, a large artificial stuffed bird that held in its claws a banner saying, SOUVENIR OF PARIS XX2.

"Just what I was looking for," Dax said.

"Is it, really?" Kira said.

"Yes," Dax said. "It really is."

"Why did you want something like that?" Kira asked her.

"I really don't know," Dax said. "I just remembered Benjamin and I had laughed about something like this quite a long time ago, and I thought it would be amusing to bring him one."

"And what about you, madam?" the clerk said to Kira. "Isn't there something you'd like?"

"I'm sure there is," Kira said. "But not right now."

When they were alone, Dax asked, "Why did you say that?"

"If she started bringing me the stuff I wanted, I don't know what I would have ended up buying. We're here to do something about Allura's luck, remember?"

"Of course I remember," Dax said.

The next incident occurred in a downtown area of the city, a place shadowed with giant monorail tracks and blank-faced office-building walls. The two officers were just walking along, not expecting anything strange to happen. Then things started happening very quickly. Suddenly they heard a siren, and a police car swept up in front of them and came to a quick stop. A young police officer stepped out, stared at them, and banged his fist into the palm of his hand—an expression of conviction on Laertes.

"I thought so!" he cried.

"You thought what?" Kira asked.

"That you were strangers in these parts. Probably aliens from off-planet. It's the only thing would account for it."

"Account for what?" Kira demanded.

"The way you were putting yourself right beside a gypsy spider moth trap and just standing there."

"And what," Kira asked, "is a gypsy spider moth trap?"

"Bad stuff," the cop said. "We don't get as many of them as we used to during epidemic season, but these creatures can still be dangerous, especially to strangers who don't know how to dispose of them."

The cop reached out and, with the tip of his billy club, poked what looked like an ordinary flowering shrub nearby. The shrub suddenly seemed to shake and shimmer and then collapsed into a large moth. Opening batlike wings, it towered above them for a moment, then shuddered and collapsed in on itself.

"This is not the usual month for spider moths," the cop said. "But occasionally you get a late survivor. It was just lucky for you that I saw the pair of you walking here toward that thing, and realized, as though by some sixth sense, that you were walking straight into a calamity."

And so the policeman saluted and went on his way, and Kira and Dax looked at each other with a look that seemed to say, "You know, there's a lot more going on on alien planets than meets the eye, especially when you aren't thinking about it much." And this was so true as to need no comment.

CHAPTER
42

KIRA AND DAX sat down on a bench in a little park. After a few minutes, Dax said, "Don't look, but do you see that guy over there by the fountain to my right?"

"I see him," Kira said, not looking. "What about him?"

"I think he's been following us."

"I've noticed him," Kira said, still not looking. "Attractive type, isn't he?"

"Not as far as I'm concerned," Dax said. "But I've never liked that sort with the cleft jaw. What do you suppose he wants?"

The man looked up and suddenly smiled. It was a brilliant smile, but a little disconcerting nonetheless.

"What do you suppose he did that for?" Dax asked.

"I think we're about to find out," Kira said. "Here he comes."

The man came over, and he introduced himself.

"Zultan Mehmet, at your service, ladies. You are both alien women, is that not so?"

"I suppose it is," Dax said, "from your point of view."

"Wonderful!" Mehmet said. "I adore alien women foreigners, and am always happy to meet them and put myself entirely at their service. That is why, once I received the signal, I turned away from the task I had been assigned to by the Romance Service and came here, where I have had the good luck to meet you."

His words were addressed entirely to Dax, who did in fact find Mehmet of considerable attractiveness.

"I don't understand what all this is about," Dax said. "What signal are you talking about?"

"It's very simple," Mehmet said. "I had a presentiment that I would meet an attractive stranger down this street, and that she and I would be very simpatico, so of course I followed my presentiment, my psychic impulse, and I met you, the loveliest thing I have seen in many a year. You were the signal, lady."

"It's nice of you to say so," Dax said. Aside from finding Mehmet physically attractive, she found everything else about him distasteful in the extreme. "Now, please have the courtesy to go away."

"But I do not understand," Mehmet said. "We are right for each other, you and I. We have both felt the attraction. Naturally there is no question of money involved. Under the circumstances, we will simply make a free gift of ourselves to each other, and both come out winners. What do you say? If you're worried about your friend, I can find someone for her, or she could wait for us at a little cafe up the street."

Dax told Mehmet in no uncertain terms that he had gotten things wrong, and that she most emphatically was not interested in him. At last, crestfallen, and still not entirely persuaded, he shrugged his shoulders and went away. Kira and Dax were able to complete their afternoon of sightseeing.

It was already obvious that the Laertians were a race of considerably psychic abilities. Even Mehmet had not been wrong in his assessment of how attractive he was to Dax.

What this had to do with Allura's winning at Andralor on DS9 was another matter. But Dax thought they were making progress, even though they had just arrived on Laertes.

CHAPTER
43

THE DAY OF SURPRISES was not yet over, however. No sooner had Mehmet gone sadly on his way than someone else approached them.

"Excuse me," a man's voice said from behind them. "I believe you were about to contact me? Or am I being presumptuous?"

Both women burst into laughter. Then Kira looked, and recognized the man. "You're Alleuvial!"

He was dressed in a lightweight tropical suit and a small peaked hat woven of straw. He looked at them in amazement, unable to see the point of their laughter.

"Yes, of course I'm Alleuvial. Did I say something amusing?"

"Not at all," Kira said. "We were laughing at a private joke. As a matter of fact, we were going to call you."

"Then it is my pleasure to anticipate you. I'm glad we meet in pleasanter circumstances than at DS9."

"You were the cause of those disturbing circumstances," Kira said, remembering Sisko's summary rejection of the ambiguous Laertian with the probable propensity toward violence.

Alleuvial smiled modestly. "Back there at the station, I was trying to relieve you of trouble rather than to cause it. If your Mr. Odo had permitted me and my friends to deal with Allura in our own way, this whole sad mess could have been averted."

"It wouldn't have been right," Kira said.

"And what is happening to you and your station—is that right?"

"Two wrongs don't make a right," Kira pointed out.

"Your superior morality almost persuades me that you are superior beings," Alleuvial said, sarcastically but in a friendly tone. "As for me, I do not care for justice in the abstract. I am a Laertian patriot, a Lampusan, but also an advocate for both our races, Lampusan and Kendo."

Kira shook her head skeptically. "You're trying to prevent Allura's party from winning the elections here. That's not what I'd call disinterested patriotism."

"It is, however. It is for the best good of all the Laertian people that the Lampusans not win this election."

"But you are a Lampusan yourself, are you not?"

"I am," Alleuvial said.

"You mean you want your own people to lose?" Kira asked.

"That is correct."

"But why?"

"There are many reasons," Alleuvial told them. "The first is that it is traditional for us to lose. Tradition is important to us."

"Even when it keeps Lampusans second-class citizens?"

"You judge without knowledge of the true situation. It is true that the Kendos, a minority on our planet, have ruled both themselves and the Lampusans since earliest recorded times. But this has come about through a free vote and reflects the considered opinions of both races. The Lampusans could easily elect a majority, but they themselves vote overwhelmingly for Kendo candidates, no matter how much their own candidates lecture them against it. Most of them feel they'll get a better deal under Kendos than under their own leaders. I can't say they're wrong."

"If that's how it is, what's wrong with it?" Kira asked.

"The Kendos have grown complacent in their long reign of power. They think they always win because they are a superior people. This sort of thinking is not only incorrect; it is also inadvisable."

"Then how can matters ever change?"

"Complexity Theory shows the way. After a long enough run of one result, the situation is primed for change. Allura's rise was predicted by Complexity Theory. The theory predicts success for her in a gambling situation. And it ties her own gambling to the results of the ongoing election. A win for her will be a win for her party."

"What do the Kendos think of this?"

"They don't pay any attention to it. It is like Kendos to think that matters will always work out in their favor. But the fact is, all of us are caught up in a case of mathematical determinism. I and a few others have gone underground, in an attempt to nip the situation in the bud and to counter the efforts of the sinister Lampusan People's Party. Your people on

DS9 have foiled our first attempt at normalizing the situation. Now we must do what we can here on the planet."

"In order for your race to remain losers?"

"Because we lose elections, that doesn't make us losers," Alleuvial said. "You know very little about this planet if you think that because the Kendos have the obvious political power, the rest of us are second-class citizens. Quite the contrary; the Kendos are so occupied with politics and art that they leave all the practical matters to us. They give themselves fine titles, but we have the money, the prosperity, the goods, the pleasures of life. We eat better than they do, and we sleep better than they do."

"If that's true, why is Allura doing this?"

Alleuvial shrugged. "She is a dissident. There have always been dissidents among us, Lampusans who are not content with having the substance of life, but want the shadow of fame and rulership, too. Can you imagine what our life would be like if we Lampusans ruled? We'd be expected to concern ourselves with political matters, instead of what we do best, getting on with life. As we gained political power, we'd be sure to lose our prosperity, as so many of the Kendos have done. In the view of most right-thinking Lampusans that's a bad swap. We've been safe enough in the past. Lampusans give so little importance to their vote that they habitually sell it to the highest bidder. Before this, the buyer has always been one or another of the Kendo candidates, since a Lampusan would never pay for what he knows is worthless. But this time, a new situation has arisen, as predicted by Complexity Theory. Allura is making an unprecedented amount of money in this damnable gambling operation, and putting it all into buying votes. She bids fair to swing the election."

"And what do you want?"

"To make her lose, and return things to the dear old status quo."

"Unlikely as it seems," Kira said, "I think that we are allies. You want to prevent an election outcome. We want to win back our station and everything that's in it, and be rid of this Gamemaster and his ridiculous rules, and his superdreadnought."

"I knew there'd be trouble when the Lampusan People's Party bought that superdreadnought. The Kendo navy was only too happy to sell it. What did they need it for? Laertes has never had a war forced upon it."

"Well, it's close to a war now," Kira said. "Have you got any ideas about how we're going to stop her?"

"Unfortunately, I do not. But I know someone here who might help."

"Who is that?"

"His name is Marlow. He's head of the Institute for Practical Complexity."

"Sounds like just the man we should meet," Kira said. "Lead us to him, Alleuvial."

"I'm afraid I can't do that," Alleuvial said. "It would put your lives in jeopardy to be seen with me. Our opposition, in this case the Lampusan People's Underground Army, have been watching me ever since my unsuccessful attempt on Allura at DS9."

"That's great," Kira said. "What are we supposed to do?"

"I will give you this padd with Marlow's address on it. You'll take a public car. I'll remain here. If the underground army is watching, they'll be likelier to follow me than you."

"Is that the best you can do?"

"Unfortunately, yes. But I beg of you. Save our

planet from Lampusan rule. It would be better for us if you took over the presidency yourself."

"No way," Kira said.

"Or gave it to someone of your choice. Please, do what you can."

It seemed like a lot of unnecessary complication to Kira, but she accepted the padd. A group of public cars came by soon after.

CHAPTER
44

SGHEEL, CAPITAL OF LAERTES, was a large city, the only really large city on the single island-continent of Alonso that made up the sole landmass of Laertes.

Sgheel played an important part in the psychic economy of the Laertians of both races. In response to obscure signals programmed in their genes, both Lampusans and Kendos from all over the planet flocked to the city between their twentieth and thirtieth years. For about ten years they lived in Sgheel, sought mates, found jobs, lived where they could and as they could. The city was a microcosm of the planet, but it was all concentrated into an area not much larger than Greater New York back on old Earth.

On the outskirts of Sgheel were the industrial parks, megablock after megablock of factories producing the goods for Laertes and for the many planets with which it traded. After the factories there was a dense belt of slums. These were situated near the factory zone, to afford easy access for the workers who lived nearby, but they were a goodly distance from the city core, where the best parks and most expensive monuments were, and distant also from the fashionable downtown streets. Downtown were the well-appointed restaurants, and the up-to-date boutiques with fashions from as far away as Earth, still supreme arbiter of fashion if nothing else. In this core area were the music halls and theaters, the amusement parks, the tasty eating-stalls with their many tempting dishes; and much else besides.

The DS9 officers had been in one of the city's finer sections, but now their car took them to the slum belt that surrounded the city like a hangman's noose around a corpse's neck, or the way Saturn's rings surround the melancholy planet. Their public car was one of the four-passenger jitneys that plied the inner city. Their driver grunted when Kira gave him the address, and made a face.

"You sure you want to go here?" he asked.

"Of course," Dax said. "What's wrong with it?"

"Nothing . . . if you're lucky." The driver pushed the lever that slid the belt over the drive wheel, and the little vehicle skidded away down the street.

The streets in the slum belt were narrow and mean, as was required by law, because no one wanted the rich to move into the poor areas just in order to save a little rent and lord it over their fellows. Municipal cleanups were limited to once a month, since it was felt that a slum area should have a certain noisome cachet to it. Livestock were encouraged to wander untended through the streets, just to make life more difficult and motivate people to go to any lengths to better themselves. Sound levels were maintained by law at an earsplitting peak; when local sounds fell below this, government noisemakers mounted on tall steel poles went into effect automatically.

A lot of thought had gone into these noisemakers. Although the Laertians were proud of their own native sounds, they were an alert and adaptive race, and they were always ready to incorporate annoying sounds from around the galaxy, all the better to irritate the slum dwellers into making something of themselves and moving to more respectable quarters. Some of the more irritating of these noise records were played on holidays.

Kira opened her guide book and looked up the entry under "Slums, Noise In." She read the entry aloud: "Here in Laertes, we try to keep the slums as noisy and smelly as possible, in order to encourage people to get out of them and make something of themselves."

"Do you suppose it works?" Dax asked.

Kira shrugged. "I suppose some get out of the slums, some don't, just like everywhere else."

"Just like everywhere."

"But in other places it's accidental. Here it's by design. It says here in the guide book that Laertes is the place that invented EFP."

"Beg pardon?" Dax said.

"Environmentally Forced Progressivism."

"I'll be sure to give credit where it's due," Dax said. "What's that?" she suddenly asked.

"What's what?" Kira asked.

"That vehicle just behind us . . . with yellow and black stripes, and the weapons hanging out the windows?"

Kira looked back, then shouted to the driver. "Get us out of here! We've got trouble!"

The driver glanced back. "We've got a pirate vehicle on our tail!" he said, gutturaling a curse, and floored the accelerator. The driving wheel spun and the belt chattered as it slipped; then the self-tightening grommets came up hard and the little vehicle spurted ahead hard. So intent had the driver been on getting up speed that he had failed to notice that he was on an intersection orbit with an orange-and-blue city garbage disposal truck coming in from the side, until Kira screamed at him, "Watch out!"

With an oath he wrenched at the wheel, and managed to strike the truck no more than a glancing blow, doing no harm to the truck but throwing the light car off course, heading straight for a wall. He tried to correct but was just too late to pull it off successfully, bouncing hard off the wall and slamming his head against one of the car's poorly placed structural members. The driver slumped back in his seat, unconscious, and the car's accelerator, depressed under his inert foot, pushed to the floor.

It was the frenzied work of a second for Kira, trained for emergencies just like this, to scramble into the front seat, push the inert driver out of the way, and grab the wheel. The vehicles were rushing along the sidewalk now, dodging people like slalom stars when they didn't dodge out of the way quickly enough.

Kira managed to get the car back onto the street. A glance at the sideview mirror showed her the pursuing vehicle still close behind. Gritting her teeth and shouting "Hang on!" she accelerated, braked hard at the last moment, and swung into a tangle of narrow little streets.

Dax had been holding on to the back of the driver's seat and studying the instrument panel in front of her. "This thing has got a radio! See if you can get the police!"

"And how am I supposed to know where that is on the radio band?" Kira demanded.

"Try that bright red spot on the dial," Dax said. "It's either the police or the dispatcher."

"Or his favorite music program," Kira muttered, but there was nothing to do at the moment but continue down the street she had chosen, since so far it was without side streets or anywhere to turn into. It was a narrow street, also, and so the pursuing vehicle, now close on their rear, couldn't pass and try to force them to a stop. Nor could it ram them, since mutually repellent electrical currents set into pulsor magnets in the bumpers of both vehicles kept them from touching—a wise safety provision. So Kira had a moment to turn on the radio and set the dial to the red dot.

The response was prompt. A gruff male voice said, "Central Headquarters, Sergeant Grob Hulka speaking."

"We need help," Kira said. "We are being pursued by a yellow-and-black striped car with armed men aboard."

"Yellow and black, did you say? That would make it a pirate vehicle. Illegal, but still used by the criminal class."

"Can you help us? This one looks dangerous."

"I wish I could help," Hulka said. "From your accent you sound like foreigners. Is that the case?"

"It is," Kira said. "We are officers from space station Deep Space Nine in the Alpha Quadrant.

"I don't know what your people are going to think of us," Hulka said, "but I can't send any units to your aid. This is one of the no-policing days for the portion of the city you are presently passing through."

"How can you have a no-policing day?"

"Such days are reserved for slum areas. They serve to remind people of the need to better themselves so they can get out of such places."

"There could be an instellar incident if you don't help us!" Kira said.

"Let's not exaggerate. If they rob you, the authorities will reimburse you."

"And if they kill us?"

"We'll do our best to bring the murderers to trial. Tell me, how are these people dressed?"

Kira glanced back and quickly described their clothing. "It's all in crimson and purple. Very garish."

"As I suspected," Sergeant Hulka said. "They're not criminals at all. Such dress betrays them as members of the Lampusan People's Underground Army."

"Can't you stop them?"

"Not allowed," Hulka said. "On Laertes, the police do not interfere with political movements. A degree of lawlessness is better than overcontrol."

Kira had no further time to argue, because the long narrow street had suddenly ended in a square with a dry concrete pedestal in the middle of it, and the road circling around it.

"Hang on!" she shouted, and spun the wheel. The vehicle rocked up onto two wheels, followed closely by the pirate vehicle. And then they were around the square and speeding into a dogleg turn.

Kira cursed and slammed in the supercharger and turned again.

It was a gallant effort, but the car failed to negotiate the tightening turn and struck a low curving wall. It was only a glancing blow, but at that speed, and given the torque of the driving wheel, it proved catastrophic. The driving wheel came loose now and cast loose its tattered and much-repaired belt. The driving wheel began spinning free and gouging the long-suffering pavement with its own adamantine image. The car tipped to one side and skidded and careened down the long curving road, people diving into storefronts and sewer openings to escape this juggernaut of inadvertent destruction. The car came into contact with another barrier, turned over and spun like a top, revolving around the single point of the liftside door handle, and broke through a series of wooden sheds piled high with copra goods, which softened the blow to the hapless inhabitants of the vehicle's interior. At last the car came to rest up against a warehouse door.

There was a moment of stark utter quiet inside the car. Then Dax shook herself and said, "Kira, are you all right?"

"I think so," Kira said. "Driver? Are you all right?"

A groan came from the front seat. The driver looked at them, his face bloody, his cap awry, and then slid back into unconsciousness.

CHAPTER
45

THE WOMEN KNEW they were in a serious situation. Leaving the driver in the car, they got out and ducked down beside a low stone parapet just before the pursuing vehicle came screaming into view. Half a dozen men piled out of the vehicle. Kira took in the situation and motioned Dax to follow her. She ducked inside the shed, fumbling with the pouch she carried across one shoulder.

"What have you got in there?" Dax asked. "A bomb?"

"No such luck," Kira said. "But I do have a phaser. It'll make them keep their distance."

"I hope so," Dax said. "What is this place?"

"Looks like a storage shed of some sort," Kira said. "Come on, let's explore."

They walked into the dark shed. It was a huge, cavernous place, with sacks of sisal fiber spun from what seemed to be a local variety of coconut. There was a set of iron stairs to one side. Kira leading, they went up them, and out a door to the roof.

Sounds of pursuit came after them. There were loud cries for them to surrender. The sky was darkening, and in the twilight Dax could see some sort of a big bug-shaped thing on the roof ahead of them.

They continued toward it, and then power-blasts flicked around them, forcing them to take cover.

"It's an ornithopter," Dax said, finally recognizing the shape in the gloom. "I'm surprised they still use those things here. But how can we get to it?"

Kira was also looking at the ornithopter. "It's a one-person vehicle," Kira said. "Look, I've got an idea. I'm going to cover you and you get into it and get out of here."

"Not without you," Dax said.

"Lieutenant Dax," Kira said, "I am your superior in rank and I order you to take that ship."

"And I'm telling you I'm not going to do it," Dax said. "If you don't like it, you can have me court-martialed."

Kira sighed. Her voice was softer as she said, "Dax, I can't make you do it, but I can ask you to listen to reason. There's a lot riding on us. We're here to save DS9 and maybe a whole lot more. I'm not trying to make a grandstand play here. One of us has to get away and solve this problem."

"Sure. But why me?"

"First of all, because I've seen you fly an ornithopter and that's one thing I can't fly. Second, because you can work with Marlow on this Complexity Theory stuff and I can't."

"And what about you?"

"This is the sort of situation I've been trained to handle."

From the other side of the roof came a man's voice. "Surrender! We will not harm you!"

"Do you believe him?" Dax asked.

"Yes. It would be crazy for them to hurt us with the power of Starfleet behind us. Anyhow, it's our only chance to get one of us to Marlow. Now get going!"

Kira stood up and began firing in the direction of the men as Dax ran across the roof and got into the ornithopter. Kira muttered to herself, "Now I suppose it won't work." But it did work. The ornithopter's antigrav unit grumbled and then came on with a rush. Wings flapping, the ornithopter, with Dax sitting in the stirrups and leaning well forward, took a short run and sailed into the air.

The wind from the 'thopter blew her off of her feet. She hit the ground, and the phaser flew from her hand. She looked up to see the men surrounding her, weapons pointed. "I surrender," she said, then waited to be blasted where she lay.

CHAPTER
46

DAX'S KNOWLEDGE OF ornithopters was mostly theoretical, although she'd once trained in one on a holodeck. The takeoff was simple enough. Turning on the antigrav unit had been simple; it was a standard module, used for many different purposes. She fitted her fingers around the wing controls, found they answered, and that was all the checkout she had time for. She ran down the length of the roof, feeling the lift of the antigrav and feeling it was too feeble to be of much use. She had always heard that ornithopter pilots prided themselves on using minimum antigrav, just enough to counteract the greater part of the effect of gravity and make the pilot equivalent to a bird.

Normally, however, ornithopter fanciers trained using antigrav units strong enough to keep the craft and its pilot in the air unaided by the wings. This, however, was a sports model, the antigrav unit barely sufficient even in trained hands. Dax could tell by the weight and the downward descent that she was going to have to fly herself out of this.

She beat the wings frantically, trying to pull herself up into the air. But the ornithopter, like a huge insect that had never learned to fly, was descending inexorably, heading directly toward a building just across the street.

"Lift, lift!" Dax gritted, and tried to bank out of the way of the building. She didn't have enough forward speed to complete the maneuver. The ornithopter began to droop, and seemed on the verge of stalling, after which it would fall to the ground uncontrolled.

She supressed her desire to beat the wings yet harder and made herself think. Why wasn't her effort producing lift? She glanced along the wings' trailing edges. They were feathered, and the lightweight plastic feathers were vibrating wildly in the wind.

That couldn't be right, Dax decided. She had read somewhere that airfoils were often controlled by adjustable surfaces located at their leading edges. Might that be the case here? Her long sensitive fingers traced the surface beneath them and found small recessed controls. At once she saw that the feathers could be set rigidly and at various angles. She set them and began pumping. The craft lifted slightly. She readjusted the angle of attack and pumped again. The ornithopter was coming up now, but the face of the building, a hulking affair of granite and red brick, was looming closer. She cut down the angle of leading edge to wing surface as far as she dared and pumped, and the ornithopter responded with full lift, almost losing its forward motion. She was lifted almost straight up in the air, soaring just over the building but threatening again to stall in midair. Just in time she readjusted the trailing edges, kicked home the tailfeather assembly, and nosed over into a shallow dive. She held it for a few moments to pick up some speed, then cautiously tried climbing again.

It didn't take her long to get the hang of it. She maintained a low altitude over Sgheel, well below the cloud layer, low enough to read street signs. A memory of the map flashed into her mind. Soon she had found Songwilder Boulevard, and followed it to the intersection of Transiger and Noyant. A left turn brought her past the botanical gardens and the houses of the lower parliament, then the gilded dome of the opera house came into view and passed behind her, and then she had located Sangunsit Street and dropped down to the ground at the very end of it, in front of the only building in the vicinity.

She stepped out of the ornithopter and walked up to the front door and rang the bell. After a short wait, a man opened the door. He was middle-aged, thickset and stocky, wearing a soiled lab gown, with a wreath of curly graying hair around his rosy skull.

Dax said, "Are you Marlow, and are you in charge of this place?"

The man nodded. "I am Marlow, and I am in charge of the Institute of Practical Complexity. How may I help you?"

"I am Lieutenant Dax, from DS9."

"Yes, of course. I have been expecting you."

"Everyone seems to have been expecting me," Dax said.

"In my case, it's natural enough. I am by way of being the local expert on Complexity Theory. And of course I am aware of your problems on DS9. But please, come in."

He ushered Dax down a long hallway and up a flight of stairs, and then down another hallway to a room that seemed to be a combination of study and laboratory. There was a desk, chairs, and a couch on one side, worktables covered with what looked like electrical equipment on the other.

"Do you know about the situation on DS9?"

"Allura's gambling? I imagine everyone on this planet knows about it by this time."

"Then you can see why we're concerned. Her successes have gone past any chance occurrence. We're in risk of losing our station. That loss could be catastrophic for you as well as us. I'm here to try to find out why this is happening and to try to do something to reverse Allura's winning streak.

Marlow looked thoughtful and concerned. From his appearance, it was difficult to say if he was a Lampusan or a Kendo.

"Interesting situation," said Marlow. "I'm sure it's related to the Theory of Complexity."

"I've heard of Complexity Theory," Dax said. "But I've never heard of it playing any part in something like this."

"That would be true elsewhere," Marlow said. "But here on Laertes, Complexity Theory is of more importance than it is elsewhere in the galaxy. It just seems to work better here, maybe because Laertians are mildly telepathic. And anyhow, this was a once-in-a-lifetime occurrence. The young mathematician, Timbo, discovered the entwined election-gambling series. It was a brilliant stroke, I grant you, but obviously he didn't look into some of the consequences when he agreed to work for the Lampusan People's Party."

"Why should there be consequences?" Dax asked.

"The theory itself predicts it. You are familiar with the n-factor trinominals?"

"Of course," said Dax.

"Ah! Well then . . ."

Soon the two were talking mostly in mathematics.

CHAPTER
47

MAJOR KIRA lay down her phaser. The occupants of the tiger car came forward as Dax in the ornithopter flapped away to safety. There were four of them, small men in dark clothing. They carried a variety of weapons, most of them antique but no less deadly for that.

Kira said, "What do you people intend? I warn you, making a prisoner of a Bajoran officer is a serious matter."

One man stepped forward. He was squat and squarely built, and there was a look of determination on his dark face.

"You must come with us. Our leader wants to speak to you."

They led her out and into their vehicle. It was a tough squeeze but they managed to all get in.

The squat man said, "I'm afraid I'm going to have to ask you to put on a blindfold." He fished a square of black silk out of his pocket.

"I don't see why," Kira said. "This is my first visit to your planet. I'm not likely to recognize anything. Except your faces, which I've already seen."

"It's protocol," the squat man said. "This is how it's always done."

Kira had lost any fear she might have had of these men. "Well, if you're sure . . ."

She slipped on the blindfold. As soon as it was in place the driver threw the lever that slipped the drive belt over the wheel and they took off, rumbling and rattling through the streets.

"Are you sure this thing is going to make it?" Kira asked.

"We hope so," the squat man replied. "If it doesn't, it's your fault because of all the stress you made us put on it during the chase."

"So sue me," Kira said.

"No," the squat man said. "That would never do."

"Why'd you have to run, anyhow?" one asked. "Couldn't you sense that we meant you no harm?"

"Maybe a Laertian could sense that sort of thing, but I can't."

"Amazing," the man says. "How do you ever know who means you harm and who doesn't?"

"We can usually figure that out without being psychic."

The car continued rattling along for what seemed like a long time to Kira. The conversation came to an end. She felt the surface of the road change from smooth pavement to what felt like sunbaked corduroy. At last they came to a stop. Kira's sense of smell picked up the odors of wet mortar, old wood, mildew, and decay.

"We're here," the squat man told her.

"Really? I thought we had just stopped for fuel."

The door opened with a squeak. She was helped out. She heard the squat man say, "How much is that?"

The driver said, "One hundred L dinars."

"So much? That's twice what it reads on the meter."

"The price is double for a kidnapping."

"Oh, I forgot." There was a clink of coins, and a murmur of conversation that she couldn't make out. Then the car drove off and they led her through a doorway, still blindfolded.

She was led down a corridor, up a short flight of stairs, around a corner and then another corner, up another flight, and into a room. There her blindfold was removed. She looked around and saw that she was in quite a large room. There were thick curtains of a dark green material over the windows, and the lighting was from overhead spotlights. In the middle of the room there was a table, brightly spotlighted. There was an empty chair in front of it, and another chair behind, in which sat a man, his features indistinct in the darkness beyond the spotlight. Kira was led to the empty chair by the squat man, who then left the room.

The man at the table leaned forward. When the overhead light struck him, Kira saw that he was a thin, balding man with small, severe features and a professorial look about him. He wore gold spectacles. He said to Kira, "I am Elgin."

"I'm Major Kira," Kira said. "Do I get some explanation for the activities of you and your ruffians?"

Elgin explained, "Dear lady, I am here as a Lampusan patriot. This is our first real chance in millennia to win an election. Favorable circumstances have combined to make this the crucial time. Our long-awaited result is close to hand. I want to implore you most earnestly to desist in your efforts to affect Complexity Theory."

"Hah!" Kira said.

"You find something funny about what I just said?"

"Pathetic is more like it. You think I'll just sit back and let Allura win our space station?"

"It is a necessary condition of the process. But I can assure you that as soon as we Lampusans are in power, we will return your station and pay any reasonable amount in damages. We need to have Allura win, but we don't need the space station."

"Frankly, the distinction escapes me," Kira said.

"What I'm saying is that you DS9 people will come out of this with a profit if you can just be patient for a few more days, maybe a week or two at most."

"And what about the anomalies that are happening all over the galaxy? Are you going to correct those problems as well?"

"We didn't know that was going to happen," Elgin said.

"You know now. How can you let it go on?"

Elgin looked unhappy, but unconvinced. "There's no way of proving that our theory is responsible."

"Maybe not in a court of law. But you know it and I know it."

"Give us just a few more days and we'll be finished. I'll even sign a document now returning your station to you."

"Forget it!" Kira said. What Elgin offered was obviously not sufficient. And also, she wondered on what authority this so-called underground leader was promising so grandly.

"That's your last word?" Elgin asked.

"Yes. Now what are you going to do?"

The leader sighed. He leaned back, and his face was

lost again in the darkness. At last, in a weary voice, he said, "Nothing."

"Now you're really lying. Or am I free to go?"

"Oh, yes," Elgin said. "You may go."

"This makes no sense at all," Kira said. "If you're going to make it that easy, why did you bother to kidnap me in the first place?"

Elgin leaned into the light again. He said, "We had to try to persuade you. But you see, it would do no good to kill you, or even hold you prisoner. Your presence is now part of the unfolding of this particular Complexity Theory problem, on whose outcome rests our welfare. For us to harm you in any way at all would make the situation all the worse for us."

"Whatever you say. I want to leave right now."

"Suit yourself. There is the door." He gestured toward a tall iron door at one side of the room.

"That's not the way I came in," Kira said.

"The other way is no longer available. You'll have to go out by the iron door. Or you could wait here until the other door is operable again."

Kira walked up to the door. Before opening it she turned to Elgin.

"If something I run into this way kills me, Starfleet will have something to say about it."

"There will be no such danger to you, lady," Elgin said. "The worst you will find behind the iron door is delay."

"Fine," Kira said. She crossed the room, opened the iron door, and stepped through.

The iron door closed behind her.

"Of course," the leader said to no one in particular, "sometimes delay is enough."

CHAPTER
48

THE TUNNEL didn't lead directly outside, as Kira had hoped. Instead, she found herself in a corridor that stretched ahead of her as far as she could see, and curved slightly to the right. The corridor was painted a cream white and was evenly illuminated by phosphorescent panels set into the walls. There was a faint odor of newly sawed wood in the passageway.

She walked for a long time, and at last came to a place where the corridor divided into three branches. A sign had been tacked up above each corridor. Each sign had sprawly black lettering. The one on the left read, PERILS THIS WAY. The middle one said, DOWN HERE LIES FROG LAKE. And the one on the right said, STRAIGHT AHEAD FOR A GOOD DINNER.

Kira stopped to think over her choices. The first question was, did these signs have any real meaning? Or were they put up as some sort of a whim on the part of her captors? If a whim, perhaps it didn't matter which one she chose. But might there be some meaning in the signs? For that matter, what were the underground people up to? Well, she couldn't just stand around and wait. She decided to pick the least ominous-sounding of them, to get some idea of what lay ahead. She chose "Good dinner," and turned in to that passageway.

The lights went out and Kira experienced a brief moment of vertigo. Then they came on again and she found herself no longer in the corridor, but in what looked like a restaurant.

She steadied herself and looked carefully. There were a dozen tables with white tablecloths, and with vases of little flowers on each table. At most of the tables people were sitting and dining, or at least eating. There was an air of calm, a sense of business as usual about the place that, given the circumstances, Kira found incredible. There was even a small orchestra seated against the far wall, a dozen men in black suits playing airs from popular Laertean operettas. A black-uniformed waiter came over to where Kira was standing.

"Ah, madam, you have been expected."

"I have?" Kira said.

The waiter smiled politely, as if Kira had made a pleasantry, perhaps even a witticism. He led her to a table, held out the seat for her, and then handed her a menu. There was a wide selection, apparently, but Kira couldn't read it, couched as it was in some obscure dialect of Laertian, probably the one spoken in Faenitas Province, where, according to the guidebook, the truffled wines were grown.

"Haven't you got a translation?" Kira asked.

"I'll be happy to interpret for you," the waiter said. "But perhaps I could offer a suggestion?"

"Go right ahead," Kira said.

"I would recommend the fish today. It is ranch-raised and mutated, in a Bajoran Katai sauce. I'm sure madam would like it."

"Fine, I'll take that," Kira said.

The waiter nodded and made a note on his pad. Then there was a sound from the kitchen door. The waiter frowned and said, "Excuse me, I must confer with my colleague."

He went to the kitchen door, talked with a tall mustached man in a tall white chef's cap, and then came back.

"Madam, I am desolated. The fish is off."

"Spoiled, do you mean?"

"Certainly not! I mean the last portion has been ordered by the archduke of Mernia-slov, considered an heir to the throne of Threska II, one of our planetary near-neighbors, who has honored us today with his patronage. Alas, I am desolated." He paused, and an idea crossed his face like a rat scuttling across a graveyard floor. "I could check and see if he has perchance changed his mind . . . the royal family is famed for their unpredictability of appetite."

"Never mind," Kira said. "I'll just take something simple."

The waiter pursed his lips, then, unpursing them, said, "The chef's doing a special on Patha eggs. Down-home style, just like on Bajor, where, I'm told, the recipe and the eggs themselves originated. For a piquant novelty, we serve this dish with Toula toast."

"That'll be fine. And by the way. Could you tell me where we are?"

The waiter had been jotting in his order book, nodding contentedly. Now he stopped, his stylus poised in the air, a look of dismay crossing his face.

"Right now, you mean?" he asked.

"Yes, of course. Right now and right here."

"That's what I was afraid you wanted to know. I'm sorry. Any questions not relating to food must be answered by the general manager."

"But I'm just asking where we are!" Kira said.

"And that is precisely the difficulty. Shall I call the manager over?"

"Yes, please do so," Kira says.

The waiter hurried away, calling out, "Manager, please! Has anyone seen the manager? We have a special situation for the manager."

Kira waited, wondering why they hadn't even served her a glass of water. Soon a man stepped out of the kitchen. He was a portly-looking gentleman in full evening clothes. His fat cheeks sported muttonchop whiskers. He had an air of haughty dignity.

"I am the manager. You were inquiring about something, madam?"

"Yes. I want to know what place we are in."

With barely a hesitation he said, "This is the famous Terminal Restaurant."

"And where is it located?"

The manager stared at her. "The waiter told me you wanted to know where you are."

"Yes, I do. And I don't see why he couldn't tell me."

"The answer to that is simplicity itself, madam. He does not know himself."

"Why is that?"

"That's rather a long story, madam."

"Never mind it, then. Do you know where we are?"

"Of course. We are at the crossroads."

"Which crossroads? Crossroads where?"

"I do not know its military or geographical designation, madam. I mean we are at the crossroads you just came from, madam."

"Yes. I know that much myself. But where is this crossroads located? What city? What street?"

"Location is not a simple matter to explain," the manager said.

"Try."

"I wish I could oblige you. But I don't know that I'm up to the challenge. In anything affecting the restaurant trade or food in general, I'm your man. But in these so easily misunderstood matters of location, I just don't like to commit myself."

"This is absurd," Kira said.

"I think the Geographer will best be able to answer questions dealing with location. Shall I see if he's free?"

"Please do so."

"It may take a few minutes. In the meantime, may we serve you with food? Drink?"

Kira realized with a start how hungry she was. How long had it been since she had eaten last? Too long!

"I already ordered the scrambled eggs."

"I am so sorry. The eggs are off. Could we offer you something else?"

"Look," she said, "I'm in a hurry. Just bring me something simple, anything that you can prepare quickly and I can eat quickly. I've got to get going."

"All our preparations take an equal amount of time, madam," the maître d' said.

"Oh . . . Bring me pestis and points," she said, naming what the guidebook says was the ubiquitous stew of Laertes. "That ought to be simple enough."

The manager hurried away. Kira looked around. The other diners were paying no attention to her. They were eating from the dishes in front of them, none of which Kira found familiar, and conversing in low voices. The orchestra had switched to a medley of

Lampusan marches. Kira waited, drumming her fingers on the tablecloth.

Soon a tall thin man with a shock of gray hair and a harried expression came out of one of the back rooms. He peered around nearsightedly for a few moments, then saw Kira and hurried over to her table. He was dressed in black formal clothes, as had been the waiter and manager. But his somber look was relieved by a scarlet cummerbund tied round his waist, and a necktie that had a red and black design.

"I believe you wanted to consult the Geographer?" he said.

"Yes, I did. Is that who you are?"

The man laughed a short, almost coughing laugh. "If only I were, dear lady, my wife might be satisfied with my position in society, instead of complaining about it all the time. No, the Geographer is in his office in the biblioteque nationale, some distance from here, pursuing his investigation of Distance."

"Who are you then?"

"I am Gregor Llunch, his second assistant. The first assistant is on vacation, I'm afraid to say."

"That's all right. You'll do fine. Can you tell me where I am?"

"That's an interesting question," Llunch said, peering at her intently. "I see why they sent for me."

"I don't see what's so complicated about it," Kira said.

"Perhaps that's because you've never taken the time to consider some of the paradoxes involved in Location. Especially the one which considers location a function of insight. The more you know about the possibilities of location, the more complicated things get. Location, you see, can be expressed in various forms: In a mathematical expression, location is

F32S by T, standing for Transformative Function, 331XEDCB."

Kira asked, "But what is that supposed to mean?"

"It means exactly what it says," Llunch said. "On the planet Hegel IV this is the customary means of expressing location."

"But we're not on Hegel IV."

"I know that very well. And I thank the Deities of Time and Location for it."

"Look," Kira said, "your explanation doesn't do a thing for me. Can't you express it in different words?"

"Certainly. The Carthusians of Ann's Asteroid would say, 'It's rablo dablo double good time when the sun's declination meets the gold of the sea.' A very nice expression, I think you'll agree."

"Very nice indeed. But what does it mean?"

"Alas, lady, I can translate expressions for you in many different languages, but there's no way for me to transmit what those expressions mean. Either you're familiar with the context or you aren't. Still . . . Maybe there's a Translator in back. Stranger things have happened." He hurried off and disappeared into the back room.

"This is very unsatisfactory," Kira said to herself aloud. "I ask a simple question and I get a runaround. I can't even get a plate of scrambled eggs around here."

Just then the waiter came running up to her table. "Good news, lady! I dreaded having to tell you that the pestis and points were off. It's a dish we've been serving nonstop since the days of the Dreadlochian Heresy, and that's a long time indeed. And then, providentially, I learned that a shipment of eggs, flash-suspended in a hiatus matrix, have just arrived from Terra. We have but to unpack them and scramble a couple and there you are. We always have toast. And we'll throw in some truffles at no extra charge."

Kira had had enough. In fact, she was beginning to suspect that something pathological was going on.

"Cancel my order," she said. "I have no time for this."

"Surely you don't mean that!" the waiter cried, his face a mask of regret. "The order will take only minutes, maybe seconds if I get it in right now!"

"I said cancel it."

Just then Llunch, the second assistant Geographer, came running back into the dining room, excitedly waving a piece of paper in his hand.

"Lady! No reason to cancel your lunch! I've got a clear-language description of your location!"

"Just tell it to me and I'll be on my way."

She snatched the piece of paper out of his hand, looked at it, turned it over, and made a face. The paper was blank.

The waiter said hastily, "Please don't judge by appearances! It's only going to take a moment or two for the information to fade in to the paper."

"Why?" Kira asked.

"There's a simple explanation. You see, when I called up this information, the computer was set for fade-in operation. That's because there are some races that use the machine and don't want to be startled by its speed of operation. So the printout comes out looking blank at first, as this one does, but then the fade-in starts to take effect and the letters come up."

"I can't wait," Kira said.

"But look! The letters are already starting to appear!"

"And," the manager said, hurrying over, "the chef

has your eggs ready for the frying pan and is awaiting instruction as to the degree of doneness you desire. There'll be some nice toasted buns on the side, of course, since we're out of toast, and your choice of mangleberry confit or olendor's chutney, both world-famous, at least around here. And I'll bet a cup of chacaka would be nice, eh? The second chef tells me that the fresh pot he's been brewing is just coming to percolation, and soon the heavenly aroma of just-roasted chacaka bean from far away Olendorf Province will titillate your sense receptors."

"And while you're eating," the Geographer said, "you will have a chance to learn your location, because the letters are definitely becoming visible now, though unfortunately in a spotty manner which will not permit reading until further development takes place. But that further development, I'm assured by the manufacturers of fade-in paper, will be of a very short duration, barely long enough—"

Kira decided she'd had enough. "Stop!" she commanded, rising to her feet. She had had a presentiment that something was very wrong here. The diners had stopped talking. Indeed, they even seemed to have stopped breathing, just like the manager and the Geographer, who stood in frozen attitudes, like actors in a tableau.

A tableau! That gave Kira the clue she had been looking for. While the manager and the Geographer had been talking, Kira had been thinking. What could account for this peculiar situation? Something was going on, but she didn't know what it was. The manager and the Geographer stood like statues, eyes fixed on her. Kira stood up and walked up to the manager. He seemed to be in a trance. His eyes weren't even tracking. She could see no sign of respiration, no swelling of the throat to indicate that breath was passing through it.

She looked around, trying to get a clue. What could it be? The scene before her eyes appeared perfectly normal. The diners were dining as before, paying no attention to her as usual. The orchestra was sawing away at its musical offerings. It was all perfectly normal. And yet, Kira felt there was something wrong.

She looked around, seeking a clue. She turned to the table nearest to her. A man and a woman were in earnest conversation. They were talking in low voices: she couldn't make out what they were saying.

"Excuse me," she said. They didn't look up.

The manager came unfrozen and said, "Madam, it is really poor form to disturb the other diners. . . ."

She ignored him. "Excuse me!" she said to the diners in a louder voice. Again, no response.

Kira reached out and tried to touch the man on the shoulder. Her hand passed completely through him.

"This is interesting," Kira said. She looked at the foods set out on their table. She reached down to pick up a small piece of purple fruit. Her hand passed completely through it.

She turned to the manager. He stepped back. But not before she reached out and tried to take his arm. Her hand passed completely through him. The manager looked embarrassed.

"You're not real, are you?" Kira said.

"No. How embarrassing for me that you found out so quickly."

The assistant Geographer said, "Look, I can explain."

"Don't bother," Kira said. "I don't need any explanations from unreal beings."

"Oh, that is unkind," Llunch said. "I'm a real person, just not a real Geographer."

Kira reached out and touched his arm. He was solid. Presumably that meant he was real.

"The others are unreal, aren't they?" she said.

Llunch nodded unhappily.

"Even the manager?"

The manager looked embarrassed, and nodded.

"This is a holosuite construct, isn't it?" Kira said.

"Yes, it is," said the Geographer. "All except me."

"And you're not even a Geographer."

"No. I'm the station attendant. I was the only one on duty at the time you entered the construct. I did the best I could to keep it realistic. But they never told me I'd have to cook, too. Look, I've got a sandwich back in the control room. If you'd like to have it—"

"Don't bother," Kira said. "I think you've used enough delaying tactics already. How long did you think you could keep me from finding out?"

"Long enough, we hoped, to keep you from interfering with the progression of this aspect of Complexity Theory."

"You ought to be ashamed of yourselves."

"Hey! All's fair in politics and mathematics!"

"That's the first time I've heard that one. Now, stop fooling around and tell me how to get out of here."

"I guess we don't dare delay you any longer. You just walk through the orchestra."

"What are you saying?"

"It's the truth. What looks like a bassoon player is actually the exit."

Kira turned away from him and walked toward the orchestra. They ignored her, still sawing away at their instruments. She reached the bassoon player and hesitated a moment. He took no notice of her. She walked up to him, and through him.

Behind him, the dining room vanished. The orchestra was gone, too. Kira found herself out on the streets of Sgheel. She hailed a public car and went on her way.

CHAPTER
49

"DAX? ARE YOU THERE?" Kira said into her communicator.

"Of course I am," Dax's voice came through. "Where have you been?"

"I was busy," Kira said. "Tell you about it later. You're with Marlow?"

"Yes. He's marvelous. We're making good progress here."

"I'll be right over."

"Kira, there's something you could do that would be of great help. I need information on the election process here."

"Right," Kira said. "I'll check it out and get back to you."

Kira took the car downtown to the city's business and financial center. Here the buildings were small and old, and crowded closely together. She walked aimlessly for a while, not sure exactly what she was looking for, letting the sights and sounds of Sgheel impress themselves on her. Her compact little guide unit, operating through a single tiny earplug, kept up a steady stream of chatter as she moved along.

"That's the Richoven Building, oldest of its type in the city. Just beyond there is the zoo, a three-star attraction, and beyond it, the Gardens of Loomis, another top attraction. Just to your left is the Lampusan People's Party Headquarters, and just to the left of that you can see Bribe Gate, where fixes are officially made. . . ."

"Wait a minute!" Kira said. "Bribe Gate?"

The translating unit took a moment to switch to response mode, then said, "That's what they call it, yes. Bribery is not against the law on Laertes, though it is supposed to be handled with a certain discretion."

"Tell me more."

"If you'd care to stroll over to Bribe Gate and ask, I'm sure they'd be happy tell tell you."

"As easy as that?" Kira asked.

"Of course. There's nothing secret about bribery on Laertes. And nothing illegal about inquiring about it, either."

Kira strolled over. She felt she was finally getting somewhere at last.

The district bribe office of the Lampusan People's Party was a disreputable-looking office building with snuff-brown walls and a sulfur-yellow ceiling. There was a row of tables, and at each table sat a district worker. One of the workers looked up and beckoned for Kira to step forward.

"Yes, what can we do for you?" the worker asked.

"I'd like to get some information on election bribery," Kira said.

"That's a big subject," the worker said. "But I can

assure you, we handle all aspects of it here. Was there anyone in particular you wanted to bribe today?"

"I'm not offering any bribes," Kira said scornfully.

"Really? Are you sure you've come to the right place?"

"Of course. I want to find out about someone else's bribe. Unless it's a secret."

"Why should it be a secret? We have all bribes on file and open to public inspection. It's required by law. Whose did you want to know about?"

"I want to know about a woman named Allura."

"Ah, Allura, of course. Our chief bribemaker. I suppose you want to write an article for one of your home-planet news services?"

"I might do that," Kira said.

The clerk was very helpful. He told Kira that all bribes were legal on Laertes, though in certain ways not considered entirely admirable. Anybody could request information about them.

"Allura is gambling on DS9 at present," the clerk said. "All indications are that she's doing very well. But that's exactly what the theory predicted, so we're not surprised."

"The theory? What theory?"

"Why, Complexity Theory, of course, in the special applications developed by our Chief Mathematician."

"Could I talk to the Chief Mathematician?"

"I don't see why not. I'll find out if he's finished his nap."

Kira waited while the clerk went off to a back room. When she returned, she was smiling broadly.

"He's up and he's just finished his milk and cookies. He'd be happy to see you. He loves to be interviewed."

* * *

The Chief Mathematician came out soon after. He turned out to be a kid about twelve years old, round-faced, a bit overweight. He was wearing baggy green shorts and a sweatshirt that said GO CHANA! Kira recognized it as an antique from pre-Cardassian Bajor that must have cost plenty.

"Are you the alien journalist?" he asked.

"There's been some mistake," Kira said. "I'm Major Kira and I'm one of the personnel of DS9."

"I know all about it," the kid said. "Is there something I can do for you?"

"You're the Chief Mathematician?" Kira asked.

"I sure am. My name's Timbo and I'm a genius."

"Do you know about the gambling on DS9?"

"I sure do. I helped set it up. Allura's doing well, isn't she?"

"That's what I've come here to talk to you about," Kira said. "How did it all come about?"

"Let me tell you all about it," the kid said happily. "But first, can I buy you a doughnut? A glass of milk?"

"No thanks, I'm fine," Kira said.

"Well," Timbo said, "the way it happened, I was playing with my computer one day and toying with Complexity Theory. That's an old doctrine here, and not too well understood. At least until I came along."

"Modest, aren't you?" Kira said.

"Hey, what's true is true. Anyhow, I found that I could set up ideal starting-points that would have predictable outcomes, with the odds overwhelmingly in favor of their succeeding. It was crazy but true. It felt like the theory itself was bending the facts of life, the physical facts. As if this theory in some way governed outcomes."

"Can you tell me what this theory is?" Kira asked.

"I already told you. It's Complexity Theory."

"And what is that?"

"It's a little difficult to explain," Timbo said, "but I'll try. I picked this up when my parents sent me to study on Earth two years ago. I was the youngest person ever to be admitted to the Institute for Advanced Studies at Princeton. What I got interested in there was Complexity Theory, which is an outcome of Chaos Theory. Am I losing you?"

"No, go on," Kira said.

"In Complexity Theory, two unrelated events may be linked and each will influence the outcome of the other."

"How?" Kira wanted to know.

"It's difficult to say in plain language what the nature of this linkage is. What would connect an election of Laertes with a particular person gambling on DS9? But they *are* intertwined, through a connection that still remains to be explicated. Though the relationship is noncausal, each is dependent on the other. A familiar example from Earth literature is the Butterfly Effect, in which the flapping of a butterfly's wings over the Amazon can, on the basis of certain conditions, give rise to a storm over Chicago. There's a connection between the butterfly's wings and the storm over Chicago. Though the flapping of the wings can't be said to have *caused* anything, it can, nevertheless, result in the storm. Say, are you sure you wouldn't like some milk and cookies?"

"No thanks," Kira said. "Please go on."

"My Earth example shows a one-way progression; first the wings, then the storm. Although the theory is true, you can't pin it down to any particular butterfly and any particular storm. But looking a little more deeply, it is possible to find simultaneous events that are linked and whose influence on each other are predictable. These events don't occur frequently, but they do arise every so often on Laertes. I was able to predict such an event for my home planet. The theory predicted a successful run of gambling, resulting in the Lampusans winning the election on Laertes."

"The theory actually predicted that?"

"Sure. It was easy enough to find it, once I knew that I was looking for. Here we have a pseudocausative linkage, but one which is really simultaneous: Allura's winning on DS9 will produce an election win for the Lampusans."

"But why?" Kira wanted to know.

"No one knows," Timbo said. "We know the links exist, but we don't know why. Getting back to an example from Earth, it's very similar to the position that early rain in the Nile delta in the spring causes good crops in the fall. The early rain, in turn, might be influenced one way or another by sunspots, or by the behavior of the Humboldt Current, or many other factors. Let's say it's the Humboldt Current, and when that strays from its accustomed course, the seagulls leave the area for better hunting grounds. Given that, we could say that seagulls leaving the area of Peruvian coast in the spring means there'll be a good crop in Egypt in the fall."

"Surely it doesn't work that way on Earth?" Kira said.

"Of course it does, but only in general terms. You can't predict the future on the basis of it. But you can here in Laertes. Complexity Theory is true anywhere, but, due to special conditions, it works better here than anywhere else in the universe. It may have something to do with Laertes' position on the far side of the wormhole, though the matter is still being studied. There's also our latent psychic ability to take into account. It may be an important factor."

"The point is," Kira said, "you saw a chance to help your people with this theory."

"That's right. And I made my ideas available to some people. And they set things up for Allura."

Kira said, "Do you have any idea what you've set loose here?"

"You mean the anomalies?"

"That's exactly what I mean."

"Well, yeah, there were some undesirable side-effects. But none of them on Laertes itself."

"Why are there side-effects?" Kira asked.

"I don't really know, but I think that, when Allura gambles, connective forces we don't know anything about are disrupted. These anomalies are a way for our universe to let off pressure, as it were, because the universe doesn't like being pushed into a corner and forced to make some particular thing happen."

"The anomalies are very serious," Allura said. "Did you consider what you were letting loose on other planets, other peoples?"

"Well, not really. I mean, I was doing pretty well just to think up the theory in the first place. And it did what I said it would. I can't be blamed for not predicting the rest of what would happen."

"You couldn't help yourself?"

"No. I was just trying to help my people."

"You like examples," Kira said. "Let me give you one from the history of Bajor. Do you know about Bata Huri?"

"Sure," Timbo said.

"One way of looking at her career is this: Bata Huri only wanted to help her people. How could she predict her soldiers would kill millions of people and lay waste a great city when she led them to the Capitol?"

"It's not really the same, is it?"

"It's exactly the same. You are a Bata Huri of science. You don't look at the consequences of your actions. You're responsible for a lot of deaths. You've ruined a lot of us by taking away our livelihood, which we're losing along with DS9. The Federation is up in arms about what is ultimately attributable to you."

"Hey, don't blame me for all that stuff! I didn't know!"

"Well, you know now, don't you?"

"Yeah, I guess I do."

"Then what are you going to do about it?"

"What *can* I do about it?"

"Help us to undo it."

"I want to help. But there's just one difficulty."

"What's that?"

Timbo looked sheepish. "I started looking into the anomalies as soon as we heard about them here on Laertes. I had a feeling things had gotten a little out of hand. I took the theory apart and put it back together again six different ways. I really worked it over."

"And?"

"And there's no way I can think of to stop what's happening. There's no way you or anyone else is going to make Allura stop winning."

"What if we removed her from the station?"

The kid shook his head. "She's already nominated several successors to gamble in her place if anything happens to her."

"Damn."

With nothing more to be gained from the Chief Mathematician, Kira left and called another public car. It was time she went to Marlow's place and found out what Dax was up to.

CHAPTER
50

WHEN HE WOKE after a few hours of restless sleep, the first thing Sisko did was wipe the sand out of his eyes and call Ops.

"Odo here."

"Any change?" Sisko wanted to know.

Odo said sourly, "Bashir is still winning, if that's what you mean."

"That's what I was afraid of. What has he won now?"

Odo glanced at a padd on which he had made notes. "His most recent successes at Andralor have won him the retracting door to the auditorium, the holoprojector that runs the star show, and several storage areas, including the one that stores the fresh fruit."

"See that someone gets the fresh fruit out of there, then," Sisko said.

"Sorry, sir. I thought of that myself, but just a little too late. The auctioneers have already taken all the fruit."

"Damn! What else has been lost in the last two hours?"

"More bits and pieces. Do you want the whole list now?"

"No, just save it for me. Is there any word yet from Kira or Dax?"

"Nothing, sir. You told us to tell you as soon as we heard anything."

Sisko signed off and thought for a moment. He considered putting in a call to Major Kira on Laertes, but he stopped himself. Kira would have called if there had been anything to report. He was just going to have to control his impatience.

He was about to catch a few more minutes of sleep when the communicator buzzed again. Odo told him, "It's Captain Adams on a priority link, sir. He wants you urgently."

"I'm coming to Ops," Sisko said grimly. To himself he added, Of course he wants me, who else would he want?

CHAPTER 51

THE GAMEMASTER stayed only a brief time on his flagship. Then he returned to DS9. Although matters were going very well indeed, there was one more thing he could do to insure success. He had come back to do it.

He walked down the Promenade, mentally adding up in his mind the value of the various things he saw. A lot of it was shoddy Cardassian workmanship. Still, it would bring something on the open market. And the armament and engine room equipment was definitely of value. The pressor beam setup and the ship's shields could be stripped out whole and sold to the best bidder; or . . .

A voice said, "Gamemaster! What are you doing here?"

The Gamemaster stopped and smiled. "Allura! I was just coming to find you! How is it going?"

Allura was looking very pretty. She was wearing one of the new gowns she had bought for this trip. The expenditure on clothing had been argued, but the Laertian People's Party, to which both Allura and the Gamemaster owed allegiance, had decided that it was worthwhile. And it seemed certain that good clothing had helped ensnare the young doctor who was doing the gambling for her.

"It's going very well," Allura said. "But Dr. Bashir is starting to balk."

"He can't do that!" the Gamemaster said. "He must continue!"

"I know that and he knows that. But I think he's starting to stall, and to make smaller bets than he had been doing formerly."

"I will speak to him if necessary," the Gamemaster said. "You must keep the game going at all costs."

Allura pouted. "It's difficult, they all want to stop. And now those ship's officers are on Laertes and I don't know what they're up to."

The Gamemaster frowned. "With a little luck, they won't learn what to do until it's too late."

"But what if they do? Can the series still be ended before I win everything?"

The Gamemaster shook his head. For the first time, a look of uncertainty crossed his face. "If we knew how to do that, we'd have no trouble at all. The theory doesn't specify, but it does identify salient external factors. On Laertes, there are four possibilities. Here on DS9, there is only one important variable. That is Sisko. He could change his mind at any time. Make us stop."

"That would ruin things for him, wouldn't it?"

"Yes. He'd lose everything, but so would we."

"Then we could blow up the station," Allura reminded him.

The Gamemaster nodded impatiently. "So we could. But even our blowing up the station wouldn't make the gambling go on. And such a move could jeopardize the election. It would terminate the series prematurely. We wouldn't get our desired outcome."

"I was afraid of that," Allura said. "There must be something we can do."

"You go on doing just what you're doing, Allura. I have a plan that ought to take Sisko out of play and eliminate him as a factor. It's a little risky, but what the hell, we have to take risks to get the result we want."

"What is it you're planning to do?"

"Nothing you need bother your pretty head about."

"But I want to know!"

"Just keep Bashir gambling. You'll see the effect of what I'm doing soon enough."

"Can't you at least give me a hint?"

"I'll just tell you this. I have a Doubler."

Allura sucked in her breath and looked at the Gamemaster admiringly. "You actually brought one aboard?"

He nodded. "It's highly illegal, of course, but I think it'll do the trick."

She gave him a sudden dazzling smile. "You *are* crafty!"

CHAPTER
52

"ARE YOU ALL RIGHT, SIR?" Sisko asked.

Adams didn't look well. The fidelity of DS9's viewing screen showed deep lines of concern in his face, and a certain haggardness around the eyes.

"This situation has given me a lot to worry about," Adams said. "Frankly, it isn't getting any better."

"What's happened now, sir?" Sisko asked.

"I'm afraid that the appearance-rate for anomalies has been increasing throughout the Federation. Two small refueling ships on the Vulcan run have been lost for no apparent reason. Luckily, they had minimum crews, so hardly any personnel have gone missing. Still, even one missing person is enough."

Sisko nodded in agreement.

"I think we've been lucky so far," Adams said. "But it can go on in this way for just so long. Sooner or later we're going to have a major catastrophe—the loss of a city, at least. Perhaps the loss of an entire planet And why should our troubles end with just the loss of one planet? As long as we don't understand what's going on, anything is possible. Already an entire mountain, Mount Babor on the planet Excelsis III, has vanished, leaving a thousand-foot hole where a mile-high mountain previously had been. Again, we've had some luck: We only lost a couple of campers and a forest ranger or two. But that sort of luck can't be expected to hold up."

"I couldn't agree with you more, sir," Sisko said.

"And the worse part of it is," Adams said, "we don't even have any way of predicting when it's going to happen next, or where. Nor could we prevent it if we did know. Civilization is catching on slowly, Commander, that something unprecedented and frightening is taking place, something that could kill anyone, anywhere. No place is safe from this anomaly."

"I know that all too well, sir," Sisko said.

"Commander, I'll remind you that the problem whatever it is seems to be originating from the vicinity of DS9."

"I'm doing what I can to correct the situation, sir," Sisko said. "I hope—"

"Hope is not enough," Adams said. "I know it's not your fault, but people are reacting in a very violent and illogical way to all this. They're looking for a scapegoat, somebody to blame, and the best one they can find is Federation command. So far we've been able to conceal the news that what's going on is somehow connected with DS9. If news of that got out, if the politicians knew or even suspected that your station was the source of their problems, the station would be in tremendous danger. The Klingons are especially enraged. Anomalies have hit them twice. They've mobilized their fleet and are looking for someone or something to fight."

"I can see how bad it all is, sir," Sisko said. "Believe me, if I had an instant solution, I'd take it."

"Solution or not, I'm going to have to do something soon, take some definite action whether it helps or not. Starfleet Command is going to insist on it. You know that, don't you, Ben?"

"I know it, sir. Frankly, I don't blame them. I'd prefer to take action myself. But when we don't know what to do . . . When we're acting blindly, just in hoping something helps . . . Well, whatever we do is more likely to make matters worse rather than better. Sir . . . Try to hold out a little longer."

Adams nodded. "That's what I intend to do. But it's not entirely up to me. Try to have some news for me soon."

"Yes, sir." Sisko hesitated. There was something he had just thought of, a favor he could ask Adams which, if granted, could win them a little more time. He hated to ask it. But he felt that as commander of DS9, he had to swallow his pride and do what he could to alleviate the situation.

"By the way, sir. I have a favor to ask. It's going to sound outlandish, but I can't explain it."

Adams seemed concerned. "This is unlike you, Ben. You know I'd do anything for you. What favor could you possibly want that you can't explain?"

Sisko took the plunge. "I want the loan of a considerable sum of money."

"Money? Did I hear right?"

"I'm afraid so, sir. I'd like it wired directly to the station. And I'd like it today, sir."

There was a long silence. Sisko could imagine Adams trying to assimilate the situation without exploding.

After a while, Adams said, in a calm voice, "You know that I can't touch official funds without at least four approvals, two Starfleet and two civilian. There's no way I can get that done, even if I could explain to them what it was for."

"I was afraid of that," Sisko said.

"But I do have certain funds of my own. My savings. Nothing spectacular, you understand. But something. Would that be of any help?"

"Yes, it would, sir," Sisko said. "I'll explain as soon as I can. And I'll get it back to you, sir. Somehow."

"I'm sure you will," Adams said. He hesitated, then said, "Commander, you wouldn't care to fill me in on just what in the Sam Hill is going on there?"

"No, sir. I wouldn't care to."

It wasn't that Sisko couldn't explain. He didn't dare, because to do so would put Adams in a position of unbearable conflict. The captain was under orders from Starfleet Command to resolve things as quickly as possible, using force if necessary. And he'd be under obligation to his own commander, as Sisko was, to let him handle things as he saw fit. Sisko was the man on the spot. He had to make the decisions. And if made them wrong, Adams had to back him up.

To tell Adams what was really going on would gain nothing except to put the captain in the sort of bind he didn't need.

"I hope to have this resolved soon, Captain," Sisko said, and signed off.

He did think this matter would resolve soon. One way or another. That's what he hoped for, and what he feared.

CHAPTER 53

BEFORE HE COULD turn away, O'Brien came rushing in. "Commander!"

"Yes, what is it?"

"The second moon of Bajor, sir—Ostratus—it's vanished!"

Sisko groaned. "Does Adams know?"

"The information has just gone out to him, as he ordered."

"I'm coming to Ops!" Sisko said.

By the time he got there, the personnel of DS9 were exhibiting signs of barely controlled panic. Adams was back on the screen, shouting mad—as if it were somehow Sisko's fault—and demanding action.

"It's all tied to you!" Adams was shouting. "All our evidence points to the fact that something connected with DS9 is at the bottom of all this. What is it, Commander? What is going on? And what are you going to do?"

Sisko was silent, struggling with what felt like an

apoplectic fit. Behind him, Odo whispered, "Sir, it's Dax. She wants to speak to you."

Adams was roaring, "Commander Sisko! I want an answer!"

"Just give me two minutes, sir. I'll be right back to you."

Sisko cut off Adams and called up Dax. She appeared on the screen, looking calm and controlled and very beautiful. Sisko could have strangled her.

"Dax! What do you have for me? What should I do?"

"Benjamin," Dax said, "I know what a spot you're in. I hate to have to tell you this. But the best evidence I can come up with just now is, you shouldn't do anything."

"That's what you called to tell me? But that's impossible! The Federation is insisting that I take action! I'm tempted to follow Odo's suggestion and put the Gamemaster in irons until this matter is resolved."

"I wouldn't advise it, sir."

"Then what am I going to tell Adams?"

Dax's patience suddenly snapped. "Tell him whatever you please! I'm sorry I don't have a nice solution for you, Benjamin, but this is how it is!"

And she cut the transmission.

Sisko felt as if a bucket of cold water had been splashed in his face. He felt an icy calm take hold of him. He was ashamed of himself. It was really bad form, shouting at Dax because he needed an answer. And it was bad form of Adams to be doing the same to him.

He hoped the captain would see it that way.

To Adams he said, "Sir, I know you need action badly. But there's really nothing I can tell you. Dax and Kira don't have any answers yet. But Dax is sure that no action is indicated now. If you want to relieve me of command and put in a more insightful commander, I'm ready to step down."

Adams glared at him, hurt and outraged, then suddenly seemed to grow very calm, as if all the wind had come out of his sails. He said, "Belay that suggestion, Ben. Do the best you can. I'll do the best I can. And, Ben . . . I'm sorry I'm hassling you. Of course you must take no action if that is the best alternative. The money, by the way, is on its way."

CHAPTER
54

IN QUARK'S PLACE, the lights were low, except for the tightly focused ceiling spotlights that were directed at the Andralor playing surface. A crowd of people had gathered to watch the play, and there were more of them arriving every day. Quark had supplied folding chairs for them to rent, and they sipped the sugary, low-octane drinks that Rom brought them, at highly inflated prices, and watched every movement of the two participants: Quark, dour and depressed, and Bashir, whose face reflected the mixed emotions of joy and chagrin. More than a few had pointed out that it was like a card game in Earth's Old West. But the stakes were higher than anything Tombstone or Dodge City had known; what was up for grabs here was an entire space station, with all its appurtenances.

People were willing to travel long distances to watch the drama unfold. Recently, Quark had begun to charge admission. People were willing to pay to watch the drama of the inexperienced young doctor who could not lose, and the wily Ferengi who could not win.

It was impossible for Bashir not to feel triumph as he succeeded at play after play, with money coming to him over and over again in double handfuls, as though by magic, or as if in obedience to his superior character and intelligence. Bashir felt godlike, and it was a good feeling.

Bashir knew that gambling, especially when you are winning, is one of the most ancient and compelling of mankind's pursuits, and one of the most addictive. Bashir knew a lot about gambling fever. He had studied it in college in the psychology courses he had taken. But his understanding of the gambling phenomenon, before the present events, had been theoretical and scholarly. He knew how ancient Gallic and Teutonic warriors, back in ancient times, had gotten so excited over the action of wagering that they bet everything they owned and then everything they could borrow. And after that, when they had lost every penny they could beg borrow or steal, some of the most dedicated punters had put their own bodies up for stakes, borrowing against their deaths when they had nothing else of value left. And when they lost that ultimate wager, they had gone willingly to the sacrifice, laying down their heads on the executioner's block, paying their debts in the only way left to them.

Julian could understand the emotion that would lead men to this extremity. He could feel it himself. He was doing nothing but winning. And the feeling was intoxicating.

But to balance off and offset the pleasure he felt at his victories, there was the dismal knowledge that he was ruining the lives of his friends and shipmates. He was taking everything from them—money, possessions, even their livelihood, as Quark grimly staked item after item of ship's property. The little Ferengi was trying desperately to hang on and wait for his luck—or whatever it was—to change. But there was no sign of that happening, no evidence that it ever would. The invisible hand of Complexity Theory hung over the proceedings, guiding the game to foreseen conclusions. Bashir was winning not because he was a good player, but because Complexity Theory was a good theory. This ruined some of the pleasure for him.

Bashir's pleasure was also marred, indeed, destroyed, by the knowledge that he himself was winning nothing. Everything he gained at the table went straight to Allura. Each time he won, he also lost, because Quark, in his desperation, was even forced to stake Bashir's infirmary, his operating theater, and all the instruments that were in it. Bashir was in a curious position: each time he won, there was less medical equipment left for him to practice his trade. A few more victories like this and he'd be out of a job.

Everyone was losing in this game except Allura.

And to make it all the worse, Bashir sensed that many people on DS9 hated him for what he was doing, detested him for always winning, and believed that if only he were really to try, he could surely find some way to lose. Bashir had thought so himself. And his confidence had been shaken when he found he couldn't manage it.

It was time for him to take a short break. Bashir put down his markers and said to Quark, "I'll be back soon."

"Don't hurry on my account," Quark said sourly.

"I'm only returning at the Gamemaster's insistence. I assure you, Quark, if it were up to me—"

Quark grunted and turned away before Bashir could finish his sentence.

Bashir was in what must be described as a state. His feelings alternated wildly between elation and depression. He could not escape the consciousness of his own guilt in this matter of such great concern to his shipmates. Obviously, a great matter was pending. Every time Bashir came out of the gambling room, his pockets sagging with currency of both paper and metal, he saw long faces around him. At first he ignored them. In his boyish glee he wanted to say, "Friends, congratulate me, I've just won a bundle. Wasn't that clever of me?"

But it is unreasonable to expect one's friends to feel good about one's winnings when they are out of those friends' pockets. That's the spot Bashir was in. He was bankrupting the very people whose good opinion he sought.

And, if that wasn't bad enough, he saw how, increasingly, Allura was uninterested in him, thought of him as little more than a cat's-paw, and cared only for the profits he brought to her.

Now, on his break, he returned to the little room near Quark's where Allura was awaiting him.

It was a small but well-appointed sitting room that Allura had had refurnished to her instructions. She was reclining on a chaise longue, when Bashir entered. She wore a gown of rose silk with three-quarter-length accordion sleeves. A single strand of dusky pearls accentuated the graceful curve of her neck, and a tendril of dark hair had crept down to just above the pulse beating softly in her throat.

She looked up and said, "What did you come away with this time? Let me see!"

Bashir opened the black bag and emptied out its

contents on a little table. Out came bundles and piles of paper currencies from halfway around the galaxy, as well as metal coins in different colors, some of considerable value. They made a rainbow display against the table's dark wood. Allura's eyes glittered as she ran her fingers through it all.

Bashir flopped into a chair. "I'm tired!" he said.

And indeed, the gambling was hard work. Especially since his motives were so mixed. When he rolled the dice now, and called out "Banco!" or "Double!" or "Suive!" or any of the other terms from Andralor that had now become familiar to him, Bashir wasn't sure what result he was wishing for.

Should he be hoping for success or failure? His failure would please almost everyone now, but Bashir still wasn't crazy about the idea of losing, not even if it was the best option. It just didn't feel right. And no matter how he reasoned, he couldn't quite get around that. Wasn't there some way he could win without having to lose first? He suspected he wasn't thinking quite as clearly as he might.

Allura took the cigarette from her crimson lips, putting it in an ashtray. Funny, Bashir hadn't even been aware before this that she smoked. No one on Earth smoked anymore. The very idea of it turned him off.

She tapped the cigarette with a crimson nail. Ashes fell like the hopes of mankind.

"What else did you bring me?" she said in a coarse voice. Funny, he'd never noticed before how vulgar she was.

"Some notes of exchange for ship's equipment." Bashir took a padd out of his pocket and gave it to her. She read from it aloud. "Section five-A of the core reactor. Number four phaser position. The rearmost wardroom locker next to the main boiler. One third of the main boiler."

She set down the papers and said in a husky voice, "You've done well, my dear. What about a little drink?"

He shook his head. "Can't drink now. This is just a short break. The Gamemaster is expecting me back in the game. Regrettably, I must return."

"That's okay with me," Allura said. "The sooner you go back, the sooner we'll clean them all out."

"We'll clean me out, too," Bashir said, rather pathetically.

"Don't worry. I'll take care of you, Doctor."

"But what of my friends?"

"They'll think of something," she said, and her voice was heartless and uncaring.

Suddenly Bashir sat up. A look of determination came into his hitherto unfocused and glassy eyes.

He said, "Allura, this whole thing has to stop at once."

"What do you mean?" Allura asked.

"You know you got me into this by a deception."

"I admit no such thing," Allura said, utilizing the impudent denial of the obvious, as Dr. Bashir knew, Paris learned to his cost when, back in Troy after his escapade in Sparta, he had begun to doubt the wisdom of his caprice with the fair Helen which had brought her to Troy and set off a world war. One legend had it that he tried to talk her into returning home to Menelaus, her husband, and doing it quickly, before Agamemnon and everybody got really bent out of shape and Achilles got into it and people started getting hurt.

The outcome was well known, of course. Helen was determined to stay in Troy, since the lady wanted an

Iliad written about her and this was the only way she could count on Homer writing one for her. It was funny how history never repeated itself in exactly the same way twice, yet always came up with what could only be called similarities, plagiarisms. Bashir only hoped Allura's tastes weren't so literary and so absolute as Helen's.

"You never told me that you were going to win all the time!" Bashir cried.

Her logic was remorseless. "First of all, how was I to know before I tried? Sure, there was the theory. But theories have been wrong before. Secondly, you never asked me. Thirdly, what's wrong with winning all the time? Is there a law against it or something?"

"I can't put my finger on it," Bashir said, "but there's something very much amiss with how you set up this whole thing. I would never have promised to continue gambling to the end if I had had any idea it was going to work such hardship on my friends."

"You didn't know how it was going to turn out, but you agreed to it anyhow."

"Well, I'm not going to stand for it any longer. I am going to quit."

"I've already told you what will happen if you do that," Allura said. "In case you've forgotten, let me just remind you that the gambling will go on with you or without you, and your friends will lose in either case, though perhaps more quickly if you are not involved."

"I know, you said that," Bashir said. "Well, I don't know whether you're telling the truth or not. But at least I don't have to be party to this any longer."

"I warn you most earnestly against quitting," Allura said.

"Hah! Why shouldn't I quit?"

"Because by agreeing to the gambling, you have put yourself in the power of the forces of Complexity Theory that control the current situation. If you try to quit now, you are very likely to pay for it personally."

"What do you mean? Is that a threat?"

"Certainly not. I am merely referring to a well-known concomitant of Complexity Theory."

"Indeed? I think you're taking shelter in a euphemism. What does 'pay for it personally' mean?"

"It should be obvious enough."

"I want to hear you say it."

"It means if you quit, you could die."

"Die? Why is that, pray tell?"

She sneered at him, her beautiful mouth twisted into an ugly sneer. "I have no time to educate you in the fundamentals of Complexity Theory as it is practiced on Laertes and as it applies to persons like yourself who knowingly or unknowingly associate themselves with the objectifications of it. The outcomes are well known, however. Suffice it to say that propinquity is tantamount to guilt in this regard, and makes you responsible for what you go along with."

"That sounds like a lot of poppycock!"

"Try quitting and see how far you get," Allura suggested, then lighted another cigarette with crimson-tinted fingernails.

Bashir could do no more than watch, abashed and discomfited, impotent to act. Although outraged, he was not ready to put his life at risk by setting himself in opposition to this ludicrous experiment. He would have to go on.

Yet even in this moment, his creative mind and adventurous spirit did not forsake him entirely. For suddenly he had an idea, and almost simultaneously the thought occurred to him that there could be another way for this to go. He didn't tell Allura what he was thinking, however. And anyhow, it was nearly time to return.

Bashir stood up and walked to the door.

"Where are you going?" Allura asked.

"There's something I have to take care of."

"What is it?"

"That's my business," he said shortly.

She looked at him—a hard look. She said, "Just remember, you have to start playing again in less than fifteen minutes."

Bashir nodded and left.

CHAPTER
55

THE YOUNG DOCTOR went to the far end of the Promenade, where some new shops had been under construction. All work had recently been suspended, awaiting the outcome of the gambling. But Sardopoulos' tent-diner was open for business, a secluded place, plain and unfashionable, that served good coffee and didn't bother making conversation. Chief O'Brien went there a lot, and, as Julian had hoped, the chief was there now, reading a novel padd.

Julian entered and walked up to O'Brien's table.

"Hi, there, Chief!"

O'Brien looked up from his book, taking care to keep his broad, freckled hand over the screen. He was reading an old Tom Mix Western and he didn't want Bashir to see it. Bashir was not only intellectually inclined; he was also a snob, and probably didn't even know it.

"Oh, hello, Julian." O'Brien slid the book into a

pocket. "What are you doing out here? I thought you had to spend all your time gambling."

Bashir forced a laugh. "It *has* become a full-time job. But I'm on a break now. How are you doing, Chief?"

"Frankly, Julian, I'm working around the clock trying to undo a fraction of the damage your antics have caused, and I'm not having a very good time at it."

"It isn't fair to blame everything that's happened on me, Chief. It would have gone just the same if it had been anyone else."

"Maybe so," O'Brien admitted. "But isn't there something you can do about it?"

"I'm glad you mentioned that, Chief," Bashir said. "That was what I was coming here to see you about. I need a favor from you. A very special favor."

"Julian, if you want to borrow money, I'm as tapped out as the rest of the crew."

"No, it's nothing like that. Money is the least of my problems. I want you to build something for me."

"A device that'll make Allura go up in smoke?" O'Brien suggested.

"Nothing so direct, I'm afraid. I want you to make a gadget for me that'll enable me to lose."

O'Brien stared at him. "What kind of a gadget would that be?"

"I'd call it an intentionality-blocker. It ought to be a device that will let me lose when I gamble."

"Do you really need a gadget to help you lose?"

"I'm afraid so. You see, as it is now, I can't seem to lose. When I try to, I win anyhow. It seems to be beyond my control to consciously make a losing move."

"What happens when you try to lose?"

"I win anyhow."

"And what would this gadget do?"

"It would register my intention to make a certain choice and enable me to do the opposite of it. To be precise, it would enable me to lose at Andralor."

The chief whistled slowly. "How could a gadget do that?"

"The way I see it," Bashir said, "Andralor is a simple game. It comes down to making a choice between an A move or a B move. No matter which I pick, I get a winner."

"Yeah, okay. What's a gadget supposed to do about that?"

"I want it to select the reverse of my intention. If I intend A, I want the gadget to tell me to pick B."

"You want to fool yourself into losing?" O'Brien said.

"That's it. I can't do it consciously, because even when I try to lose, I win. But with the proper sort of gadget . . ."

"Hmm," O'Brien said. "A gadget like that would have to be able to read your mind, wouldn't it?"

"Not exactly. Intentionality is registered in the nerves and muscles. Before one performs an action, there is an unconscious set toward doing it one way or another. That's elementary first-year medical stuff. So if you could develop an instrument that registers which way I'm likely to choose in any given situation—something I don't even consciously know myself—and then lets me perform the opposite of my intention . . . Well, that should do it nicely."

"I think I get the idea," O'Brien said. "But if you used something like that, that would be cheating, wouldn't it?"

"Not at all. I have as good a right to gamble and

lose as I have to win. I just need to be able to make a choice between winning and losing, not be merely bound up in it."

"If you say so," O'Brien said. "I'll see what I can do. But don't you have to get back to the play?"

"Yes, I do," Bashir said. "Do try to hurry, Chief. Before I win everything in sight and end the game that way."

So saying, he turned and went back to Quark's Place, ready for the next session.

CHAPTER
56

CHIEF O'BRIEN went to his workshop. His mind was filled with a vague but compelling conception for the device Bashir needed. There was little in the world O'Brien liked as well as tinkering, and so he hummed to himself as he put together the device he had visualized. A portable circuit case, gutted long ago, served as the shell. An old potentiometer, modified slightly, which he needed as the heart of his device, fitted well into it. Other things were needed. O'Brien found them and fitted them in, still humming. Then he tested the result, made adjustments, tested again, adjusted again, and finally, after some repetitions of this, decided the gadget was ready.

It was some hours later when Chief O'Brien left the workshop and went down one of the back corridors, then through a side connection. The lights had gone out in this section of the station, but he moved unerringly in the dark, continuing with scarcely a pause or hesitation until he came into the light again. No one knew DS9 like he did.

Soon he was near the Promenade. He got there just as Julian Bashir was returning for another stint of gambling.

Julian said, "Have you got it for me, Mr. O'Brien?"

"I have indeed." The chief drew something out of his pocket that looked like an antique Walkman radio. It had several leads with sharp points.

"Put this into your pocket. The leads are spring-driven. Just press this button and they snap into your skin at the thigh. The rest is automatic."

"Will it work?" Bashir asked.

O'Brien shrugged. "I hope so. It's the best I can do, Julian."

"I hope so too," Julian said "There's not much more of the station left to lose. And collection time is coming right up."

CHAPTER
57

CHANGES HAD BEEN MADE in Quark's Place just in the short time since Bashir had last been there. The room had been increased in size by knocking out one wall and taking over the storage area behind. This had given room for several more rows of seats in the new space. Each seat had a number affixed to it, and Ferengi dressed as ushers were leading ticket-holders to their seats.

Quark was discussing details of the evening's dinner with his staff. Quark reminded his help that there was a choice of five dinners tonight, one for each of the major food-taste areas in the Gamma Quadrant. There were to be no substitutions, and a pickle counted as a green vegetable. With this taken care of, he moved to the Andralor layout, where Julian was awaiting him.

Bashir said, "Quite a crowd tonight. But I didn't know you were selling seats, Quark."

"What do you expect me to do? Let them watch without charging them? Not a chance! And did you notice the cameras?"

Bashir hadn't. But following the direction Quark indicated, he saw two large cameras mounted on dollies high above the crowd.

"What's that for?" Bashir said.

"I'm selling galaxywide viewing rights."

"Very enterprising of you. What are you doing with the money you get?"

"What do you think? I'm using it to play against you. And I'm still losing!"

Bashir was touched in spite of himself. "Quark, I can't tell you how sorry I am about this. If there were only something I could do about it . . ."

"I don't want to hear it," Quark said through gritted teeth. "Shall we begin?"

Bashir settled into his seat. Before he could place his first bet, he found a young woman standing beside him, with two others just behind her. They were young, pretty, and obviously Laertian.

"What can I do for you?" Bashir asked.

The foremost, a stunning redhead, said, "Hi, I'm Mona. I'd like an autograph. Me and my friends are fans of yours."

"Really? You're not kidding me?"

"Definitely not. You're the hottest number that's come near our planet since it was created. You're a dead cool gambler and we like that."

"All our friends like it, too."

"You've become a cult hero, Dr. Bashir."

"Is that a fact?" Bashir said.

They looked at him expectantly. They were young, fresh, charming, and naive. Bashir found himself with an unusual sensation: he felt old, stale, gruff, and cynical.

"Well," he said, "you'd better go away, I have work to do."

They giggled at each other. Mona said, "Let us stay. Afterwards, we'll all party."

"Party?" Bashir said.

"I'm sure you know what I mean."

Bashir was tempted. It had been a long time since he'd had any fun. It had just been work, work, work, for what felt like weeks, though it was only a few days since this gambling thing had begun. To party with these girls . . . but no, he reminded himself he had a job to do.

"Thank you all very much. Now, please get out of here!"

They left. Bashir settled into his chair and started to gamble.

At first he tried to lose in the usual way, on his own, without having recourse to O'Brien's device. But it was no use, he just couldn't lose for winning. He reflected to himself that when you're good, you're good, and he was obviously good because his every move was a winner.

During a brief lull in the play Bashir touched a switch on the side of the radio in his pocket. He felt the switch make its short travel and click into On position. There were two pinpricks as the leads went through the fabric of his trousers and inserted themselves into his thigh. At the same time, reaching into his other pocket, he injected himself with the one-shot hypospray he had prepared earlier. Filled with a drug to improve nerve-transmission in humans. That ought to help O'Brien's device.

Quark must have caught some movement. "What's the matter?" he asked.

"Matter? What should be the matter?" Bashir riposted.

"You're squirming around like an eel with the itch," Quark said.

"I had Garak take in my uniform a while back," Bashir said. "I think he took it in a bit too much. Are you ready?"

"As ever," Quark said dourly.

The two returned to the Andralor table. Bashir made a bet. Quark hesitated.

Bashir asked, "Are you calling my bet?"

"Yes, of course I'm calling," Quark said. He peeked at the two down cards that had come flying to him out of the flat sandal-like device called "La Zapata" by the Catalan merchant-playboy who had invented it.

Watching intently, Julian saw that Quark evidently liked what he saw. The little Ferengi grinned and pushed a pile of chips into the center of the table. "Your move, Doctor."

Bashir could feel the warmth and numbness spread from his thigh throughout his body, the effects of the neurotransmitter.

Running counter to the drug, like a series of little waves running across the tops of bigger waves, was the electrical coding of O'Brien's device, opening up for Bashir a full and complete knowledge of what he was about to do, and with it, the strength of perversity necessary to do the opposite of what he intended.

"Your move, Doctor," Quark said.

Bashir knew what move he needed to make in order to lose. His hand reached out, seemingly of its own accord, and arranged two markers. Then he smiled and sat back.

The silence in the room was so deep you could have baked a cake in it and still had enough left over for a plate of latkes.

A sigh came up from the crowd. They didn't know

what they were reacting to; but they knew something strange was happening.

"I don't know how you did that, Doctor," Quark said, pushing a pile of bills and markers toward him. "I thought I had your play figured out for sure. And then you ran counter to my expectations. How did you anticipate me?"

Bashir knew it was bad luck on Quark's part that he had changed his strategy at the same moment Bashir had changed his, thus in effect canceling out Bashir's hoped-for result.

"Why did you pick this time to change your strategy?" Bashir asked.

Quark shrugged. "Why did you pick this time to change yours?"

Bashir wouldn't have been a bit surprised if a voice had opened up a mouth on him and said, "There is no such thing as free will. Whatever happens is covered under Complexity Theory." No such thing happened, but Bashir was sure that that was the reason. Complexity Theory had anticipated him, and adjusted the game accordingly.

Well, he had tried. He said to Quark, "Shall we continue the play?"

Quark shook his head. "I have nothing left to wager."

The Gamemaster had been reading in the back of the room. Now he stood up and said, "I will declare a short recess to give Quark time to come up with more money or collateral."

"It's all gone," Quark said. "You've got it all."

"See what you can do," the Gamemaster said pleasantly. "If you really can't continue, I'll have to declare the game over and award the station and everything that's in it to Allura."

Stunned, Quark turned away. And then Rom was there, pulling at his sleeve.

"Yes, what is it?"

"Commander Sisko wants to see you at once."

"I expected as much," Quark said. "Is it going to be a firing squad, or are they merely going to hang me?"

"Brother, what are you talking about? Get control of yourself!"

"Yes," Quark said, straightening his back and squaring his puny shoulders. "Let it never be said that Quark went to his death with anything but contempt for his enemies."

Rom shook his head as Quark marched off to face the commander whose space station he had lost.

CHAPTER
58

QUARK WALKED down the corridor on his way to Sisko's quarters. Before he could reach it, his brother Rom came racing up behind him.

"Quark! Wait!"

"Go away, Rom," Quark said. "This is something I have to do by myself."

"I wasn't planning on going in with you," Rom said.

"Then what is it?"

"You must not go to the commander."

"Oh, really?" Quark said. "What would you have me do instead? Hide?"

"That's exactly what I was thinking," Rom said.

"Impossible. Odo knows this station like the back of his hand. I really don't want that shapechanger dragging me away."

"I wasn't thinking of hiding on DS9," Rom said.

"You have something better in mind?"

"Yes. I have made arrangements with the captain of

a small trading vessel. He has agreed to take you and me to a place of safety. You see, I've been thinking of you, brother."

Rom looked very pleased with himself.

"You've been busy, haven't you?" Quark said.

"Indeed I have, brother. I have remembered a Rule of Acquisition."

"Which one?"

"The one that says a Ferengi must guard his own lobes by guarding his brother's lobes."

"I don't remember that one."

"It was expressed in more elegant language. But the meaning is the same."

"So you arranged all this without telling me?"

"Yes, of course," Rom said, puzzled. Quark wasn't taking this the way he'd expected him to. He had been expecting gratitude, not this cold stare.

"I've done it to save your life," Rom pointed out.

"And your own, of course."

"Of course. That's the point of the proverb, you see."

"And does your proverb also tell you how you were going to pay for this escape? I'm broke, in case that escaped you."

"I did notice," Rom said.

"And you're broke too, right?"

"Well, not exactly."

"Perhaps you'd care to explain."

"A different Rule says that when stormy weather comes, the wise Ferengi will put something aside so his lobes don't get washed away. Those aren't the exact words, but the meaning is clear enough."

"So when I asked you the other day for a loan, and you said you had no money, you were lying?"

"Well, not really lying. Exaggerating slightly, perhaps. I gave you everything but my rainy day fund. I suppose you have some emergency currency put away, too?"

"No, I do not," Quark said. "I've staked everything I had on the game. And everything anyone else had, too!"

"I thought as much," Rom said. "That's not up to your usual standards of deceit, brother. It's lucky I was looking out for both of us. Come, let's be off before Sisko sends Odo after us."

"Don't be ridiculous," Quark snapped.

Rom stared at him in disbelief. "Brother, have you taken leave of your senses?"

Quark said, "I daresay I'm as suspicious as the next Ferengi. But I cannot believe that Sisko means me any harm. He knew what I was doing. And he approved it."

"Approved?"

"Well, he went along with it."

"Yes, of course," Rom said. "But that was when he still thought your plan had a chance to save the station and make him rich. But now that everything is lost and the end is in sight, what is there for him to do but make you the scapegoat?"

"That's what you or I would do," Quark said. "But not Sisko."

"You think he's better than we are?"

"Not better. Just different. What you suggest is simply not a conceivable action for our noble commander."

Rom wanted to tell Quark that he was getting feebleminded. But he softened it and said, "I think you're losing your marbles, brother. If Commander Sisko is not holding you accountable, why has he signaled *Bellerophon* to come here at warp speed?"

"The *Bellerophon* coming here? Are you sure?"

"I have advance notice from a fellow I bribe in

Communications. The *Bellerophon* is due here at any moment."

"And Sisko sent for it?"

"Why else would it be coming here? Obviously, Sisko has had enough. With *Bellerophon* here, he'll vaporize the Gamemaster and his stupid super-dreadnought and arrest you for consorting with the enemy. Come, we can still get away."

"You go if you want to," Quark said. "I think you've misread the situation. I'm going to see Sisko. Whatever he has in mind, I'm sure I can talk him out of."

"But brother, you've lost all credibility!"

"Especially with you, eh, Rom?"

Rom hung his head. "I'm your brother. I'm trying to save you. And I still believe in you."

"If that's the truth, get a refund from whoever you paid and bring me the money. Then go back to the bar and see that everyone has drinks. I'll be along soon."

"And if you don't come back? What if Sisko, in a rage which I consider entirely justified, strikes you down on the spot?"

"Then everything I have is yours. Too bad it's only debts."

And Quark turned and walked on down the corridor.

CHAPTER
59

ROM WENT TO a communications console in his quarters and called the captain of the ship he had contracted for. As he had feared, the captain was more than willing to let the rescue mission pass, but he refused to refund Rom's money.

"It's barely an hour since I made my arrangement with you," Rom pointed out.

"With me, deposits are nonrefundable. If you don't like it, take me to court."

"If you're going to keep my money, then you have to perform a service."

"I told you I was willing to do that. It's you who've changed your mind."

"No, I'm merely delaying my decision. I'll let you know when we're going and where."

"I'll be around," the captain said, "unless, of course, I'm elsewhere." And with that Rom had to be content.

He returned to Quark's and sat down disconsolately in one of the chairs. It was a break in the moment's action, with Quark off seeing Sisko, and Bashir freshening up. Rom decided it was time for him to get very drunk. It wouldn't solve anything, but it would make him feel better. He was just reaching for a bottle of overproof Kenukian rum when he noticed someone standing outside the entrance.

"Come in," Rom said.

In walked Olix, the Ferengi priest.

"Hello, Father," Rom said. "I thought you were off visiting other Ferengi far from home."

"That was my original intention," Olix said. "But I decided instead to stay here. This situation is too interesting to miss. And I do have a hundred GPL bars riding on the result. How *are* things going?"

"Terribly," Rom said. Then he got control of himself and added, "For Allura and the Lampusans, I mean."

"That is good news indeed," Olix said. "Are you close to breaking her yet?"

"Very close indeed," Rom said. "That is the next phase of the operation, known, technically, as the Kill."

"Excellent. And what comes before that?"

"Before that," Rom said, "we finish the present operation."

"And is there a technical name for that, too?"

"Yes, Father. It is called Fattening the Pot."

"Ah, of course. That requires some strategy, I daresay."

"Indeed it does," Rom said, extemporizing furiously. "It requires lulling the young lady into a false sense of security, and getting her to wager larger and larger amounts, which will bring us even greater winnings when we pull the switch."

"The Switch? Another technical term?"

"Even so, Father."

"How happy I am to be sharing in this coming windfall, even if it is to a minor extent."

"We're happy to have you aboard, Father. It would still be possible for you to increase your stake in this brilliant and quintessentially Ferengi operation."

"If only I could," Olix said. "But that latinum I gave your brother was the entirety of my savings. We priests of the Charismatic Fathers of Profit and Loss need no money. Our Order takes care of all our expenses."

"Perhaps the Order would care to participate in this windfall," Rom suggested.

"The Order? You are referring to my Order?"

"Exactly," Rom said. "Why should not organized religion profit as well as private enterprise?"

"I never thought of that before," Olix said. "But you're right. This is just the sort of pious work the Charismatic Fathers would be interested in."

"Why not contact them at once?" Rom suggested. "I have a communication device right in my quarters."

"Yes, I'll talk to them," Olix said. "But my conversation must be private. No offense, my dear Rom, but the interior communications of the Church are not for the ears of outsiders."

"I'd hardly consider myself an outsider," Rom said. "But of course it will be just as you say. My quarters are nearby. The communications console is on the desk. You know how to use it, I presume?"

Olix laughed. "My son, we are not so unwordly as to not know how to use a simple device like a communicator. Wait here. I'll be right back."

The Ferengi priest went to Rom's quarters and

closed the door. Rom considered listening in, but decided against it. There might be a hum in the transmission, and that could ruin everything.

He sat, drumming his fingers on a table. If this didn't succeed, he didn't know what he would do. He had already tried to borrow from members of his own family. They had been rude enough to laugh at him.

The wait seemed long, but was probably no more than ten or fifteen minutes. Then Olix returned, and he was beaming.

"I explained it all to the Father Superior," he said. "Lucky I caught him just before he was going on a tour of shrines of Priests Martyred for Money. It is something the Father Superior does every year, and it is a most moving ceremony."

"I'm sure," Rom said. "But what did the Father Superior say?"

"Because of the pressing circumstances, he made a snap decision. Very unusual for him. He agreed to invest in the venture. But there are strict conditions."

"Of course," Rom said, beaming. "How could it be otherwise? We'll draw up some documentation now. How much was the Father Superior willing to invest?"

"Fifty thousand bars of latinum," Olix said, his eyes growing wide as he mentioned the sum.

"A very useful amount," Rom said.

"But there are conditions!"

"We'll set those up right now," Rom said. "I suppose the Father Superior is wiring the money by subspace? Excellent, excellent!"

CHAPTER
60

"COME IN, Quark, come in."

Quark entered the commander's quarters reluctantly. Despite the brave front he had shown to Rom, he was none too sure what Sisko's attitude would be, or what he wanted. Now that he thought of it, he really didn't know Sisko at all. The man was as strange to him as a Lemurian tridonc. Perhaps the commander had been brooding over his losses, and had driven himself into a murderous rage. It was hard to tell with quiet people like Sisko.

But Sisko didn't appear to be in a murderous rage, or even especially upset. He was sitting at his worktable. The lights were low. Soft music was playing in the background. Quark found so peaceful a scene as this disquieting.

"Take a seat. How's it going?"

Quark sat down. He thought of several roundabout statements, then decided to take the plunge.

"Very badly, I'm afraid." He took a deep breath. "As a matter of fact, I'm wiped out."

Sisko nodded matter-of-factly, as if he'd been expecting to hear this.

"I was afraid of that. What does the Gamemaster say?"

"He's allowed a short recess to give me time to raise more funds. Very shortly I must either continue play or forfeit everything."

"Everything?"

"Yes, sir. Everything."

"I was afraid we had reached that point. So this comes at a very convenient time."

Sisko took a padd from his desk and handed it to Quark.

Quark looked at it. It was a bank transfer order addressed to Sisko and crediting him with a hundred thousand bars of GPL.

Quark asked, "Where did you get this, sir?"

"Never mind. I've endorsed it and it's good. That's all you need to know."

"But what is it for?"

"That should be obvious. It's for you to continue gambling with."

Quark turned the padd nervously in his hands. "Commander . . ."

"Yes, what is it?"

"I think it only fair to tell you that my luck—well, it isn't working very well at present."

"That is evident," Sisko said.

"So this money, sir—well, I appreciate the gesture, but might you not be better off keeping it yourself?"

"For a rainy day, you mean?"

"Yes, something like that."

"That rainy day is here, Quark, as I'm sure you've noticed."

"I agree. But to throw good money after bad—"

"Quark!"

Quark sat up straight. "Yes, sir?"

"When this thing started, you told me that you could win. You said the house advantage was an eternal truth. You said that you understood gambling, you knew your own skills, and in the long run, you had to win."

"Well, yes, I did say that, but—"

"But what?"

"But it hasn't happened, Commander! I'm wiped out, and I've lost the station!"

"That's just because we haven't reached the end of the long run," said Sisko.

Quark's face showed the presence of an unaccustomed emotion. The Ferengi didn't have a word for "admiration," but that was what Quark was feeling. Only temporarily, of course. He'd soon return to his senses. But for now, he was in awe of Sisko.

"Commander," Quark said. "Are you saying you think I can still win?"

"Look at it this way," Sisko said. "I've got Lieutenant Dax and Major Kira, my two best people, trying to find an answer to this. And I've got you, Quark, my best gambler, holding the situation together until we can do something about it. Our position is grave, but by no means hopeless. What is important here is not to lose faith in ourselves, Quark."

Quark stood up. His hands were trembling. "Thank you, Commander. You've brought me back to myself. I'll manage somehow. I'll buy you some more time."

"I know you will," Sisko said.

Quark moved to the door. "Maybe we won't need the *Bellerophon* after all."

"What are you talking about?"

Quark realized he had been indiscreet, to say the least.

"Just a rumor, Commander. I don't really know . . ."

A communication light on Sisko's desk console flashed red.

Sisko pressed a light-sensitive spot on the console. "What is it?"

"Ensign Blake, sir. The *Bellerophon* has just been spotted by long-distance sensors. Captain Adams is signaling for a talk with you, sir."

"I'll be right there." Sisko signed off and turned to Quark. "I won't carry this any further with you, Quark. I have business to attend to. And so do you."

"Yes, sir." Quark reached the door. It dilated ahead of him.

"Oh, just one more thing."

Quark stopped in the doorway. "Sir?"

"Whoever your informant is in Communications, you might tell him it looks better if he gives important signals to the commander before passing them on to his bribemaster."

Quark nodded and exited. He was planning on having a word or two with Rom. The fool hadn't even set up his bribe properly!

He hurried down the corridor toward his place. It occurred to him that Sisko was handling this very well. And as he walked, the beginning of a plan began to form in his mind.

CHAPTER
61

THE *BELLEROPHON* was soon within visual range of DS9's sensors. Benjamin Sisko thought he had never seen so fine a sight as the large starship hanging in the black of space. He couldn't take much pleasure in it now, however, since he knew it had come in response to problems in his station. On a personal level, this could mean a black mark in his service record. He was only slightly relieved when Captain Adams began their conversation on a mild, almost apologetic note.

"Ben? I'm sorry to come charging out to your command area this way. It was a Starfleet decision to send *Bellerophon* here. I protested, but I was overruled."

"Yes, sir," Sisko said. "Are you here to take over?"

"Not at all! I told them I would have nothing to do with that."

"But the suggestion was made?"

"Not seriously. It's the sort of thing top brass thinks

about when things don't go as they think they should."

Sisko didn't remind Adams that the captain was one of those dissatisfied top brass.

"Officially," Adams said, "we're here on a training mission."

"And unofficially?"

"Well . . . We're here if you need us, Ben."

"Yes, sir," Sisko said, and waited.

Adams cleared his throat. "We're also here to intervene if Starfleet decides the situation is getting out of control, or requires resources beyond your power to command."

"I understand. You're saying, Get this situation squared away or we'll come in and do it for you."

"Ben, that's unkind. What would you have Starfleet do? Stand around and wait until we've lost something really important, like Luna, or Earth, or even Sol?"

"I understand it's a tough situation all around. If you think you can do any better—"

"Belay that, mister! I have complete confidence in you. You have received tangible evidence of that, I believe."

Sisko knew Adams was referring to the transfer of the hundred thousand credits. He knew Adams had gone out on a limb for him. But he couldn't get much enthusiasm in his voice as he said, "Yes, sir. It was very much appreciated."

"Ben, isn't there something you can tell me?"

"Nothing that would help, sir."

"Any results from Dax and Kira yet? Is there anyone we can send in to back them up?"

"Take over from them, you mean?"

"Take it easy, Ben. You're getting very touchy."

"Dax has just called in. Shall we make it a three-way conference?"

"Yes, let's do that."

Dax, on Laertes, came into the conference with Sisko on DS9 and Adams on *Bellerophon*. Formal greetings were exchanged.

Sisko said, "Lieutenant Dax, Captain Adams wants to know if he can assist you in any way."

Dax's reply was silky and controlled. In her various host bodies she had been reading inferences for too many years to let this one pass unchallenged.

"If there's any doubt about my abilities or my loyalty, Captain, it would of course be your duty to replace me at once. I assure you, I will understand."

"Damn it all, what's everyone getting so excited about?" Adams asked.

Dax said, "No one's getting excited but you, Captain. If you have any doubts about me, now is pretty late in the game for you to be expressing them."

"I'm sorry, Dax," Adams said. "It's just that this situation is so frustrating. . . . Look, I know you think a lot of your theories. Under any ordinary circumstances, I wouldn't be considering overruling you. If I do, I can assure you it won't be because I have any doubt of your loyalty or ability. But the crux of the matter is this: These people, with their superdreadnought, are trying to force us into a certain course of action. Maybe they could do that when we had no force with which to oppose them. But now it's different. I'm out here with the *Bellerophon*."

"Force will do us no good in this situation," Dax said. "They know it, too."

"I think they're bluffing," Adams said.

Dax said, "It doesn't matter if they're bluffing or not. It's not their strength of arms that's holding us back, it's the situation according to Complexity Theory."

"That theory," Adams warned them, "is still under discussion as to whether it has any truth in it or not."

Dax said, "But there's no time for discussion. We're in the sphere of influence of Laertes, and here Complexity Theory is very important indeed."

"So what are they going to do to us?" Adams said. "What can they do if we tell them to clear off DS9 and wait until we've sorted things out."

"Sorting things out is what Marlow and I are trying to do," Dax said. "As to what they will do—probably nothing. But if you fly in the face of the theory like this, you can expect more anomalies. And in that case, I doubt if we'll ever see the moon of Bajor again, to say nothing of the other stuff that's gone missing."

"Damn it," Adams said, "I wasn't sent here to temporize!"

"Of course not," Sisko said. "You've got me here on the spot doing that for you."

"Now, Ben, I didn't mean it that way. What I'm saying is, the Federation Security Council sent me out here to do something about this situation. Make or break, but stop backing down!"

"Sir," Sisko said, "I operate under essentially the same orders as you do. Might I suggest you bite down on the bullet as I've had to do and give Dax a little more time?"

"You mean do nothing?" Adams said.

"That's exactly what I mean," Sisko said. "There are times when no action at all is the best action."

Adams was silent for a while. Then he said, "Dax, how much more time do you need?"

"It's impossible to say for sure," Dax said. "But Marlow, my associate here, thinks the situation is going to break one way or another very soon. There are a couple of things we are going to try. They're pretty desperate measures, but the situation calls for them."

"What are you going to try?" Sisko asked.

"Marlow and I have a plan. We just want to do some more checking before we put it into effect."

"Do you think it'll work?"

"At least it'll give us a chance."

And Adams had to be satisfied with that.

CHAPTER
62

MARLOW HAD a magnificent bush of wavy, iron-gray hair, which he tossed back like a lion's mane. His face was deeply cut with the lines of living. His hands were big, with blunt fingers. But they handled the instruments with surprising delicacy.

Dax and Marlow were in Marlow's laboratory. It was an old place with curving masonry walls and ceilings. Fluorescent lighting bathed everything in a sickly greenish glow. Marlow was tapping out data on the computer. He was a virtuoso on the instrument. He was in constant motion. One of the dancing Kendos, Dax learned later. The whole species was characterized by being in constant movement.

From the first moment of Dax's arrival, Marlow had been eager to help. A Kendo of an old and proud family, he didn't want to see the Lampusans take over the government. And the anomalies taking place throughout the universe bothered him deeply.

"These anomalies," he told Dax, "are bad signs.

There's something wrong with Complexity Theory if it can produce results like this. Something that could almost be considered evil. I suspect it's an alien theory, trying to muscle its norms into our universe. Things like this shouldn't be happening. This is nature's way of telling us to stop tampering."

Dax didn't buy Marlow's theory of an evil alien intelligence working through sinister mathematics. But she agreed that the situation had to be changed. If that was possible.

"Of course we can change it," Marlow said. "I refuse to believe this is a predetermined situation with only one outcome. We already know there are no such things. All is in flux. Nature follows the law of averages. That's nature's way."

"Not always," Dax said.

"True. There's Exceptionality, of course; has to be, otherwise we'd be living in a completely deterministic universe, a universe such as the one described by your Isaac Newton, where each action determines the next, and the whole series of actions can be traced back to a single original source. I'm saying that that is exactly the sort of thing that can't happen."

"It is happening," Dax said.

"Only apparently, not actually. This Complexity Theory run is a long exception to the rule that averages will out. But I tell you, Dax, nature herself desires us to solve this problem, to cure this anomaly-making horror that all the other anomalies are mere shadows of. We have to solve it. Because if anomaly becomes the rule, as will be the case if this series is allowed to run out unimpeded, then that becomes the rule for the universe."

"I always thought the universe could take care of itself," Dax said.

"The universe has one strange habit. Although it's

for the most part steady, self-sufficient, and reliable, it does have a propensity toward trying out new things. I know this is an anthropomorphic way of looking at matters, but bear with me. We know that the universe is forever experimenting with its own rules by throwing up exceptional situations. Either they become the rule or they become anomalous. The present universal setup, the one we know, is the one that has succeeded best so far. We live in a universe in which short-run anomalies are possible, even necessary, so there can be the introduction of the new, the antideterministic. But it is also necessary that these anomalies run out, end, and matters return to the steady state."

"How long will it take for the this set of anomalies to work themselves out naturally?" Dax wanted to know.

"We can't say, with our limited perspective, what is long and what is short. It seems to me, though, based on my lifetime's experience, and the lifetime experience of other scientists whose deductions I have read, that something like this, this gambling series in which against all odds one side always wins, and in which this winning means that a party that can't win political power *must* win—has been going on too long to be merely anomalous. It's tending toward the normative. It's become an experiment of nature's, to see how this rule plays in the universal arena."

Dax waited for him to go on.

Marlow sighed. "We like the universe the way it's been set up. The rules worked pretty well for us living creatures. The present setup makes planning possible, makes rationality work."

Dax asked, "You think you can get nature to change its mind about this change?"

Marlow shook his head. "It is presumptuous to think of improving on nature, but that's exactly what we're trying to do here. Only it's not so much an improvement as a return to how things were, a move away from the chaotic conditions that threaten to snap into being if this goes on. That is why I will work with you, and why I feel the urgency I do. We must get this thing solved."

Marlow went to work immediately. But he didn't explain much at first. Dax had to ask him, "What are you doing now?"

Marlow said, "I'm running the Sigma Series again. This time I'm transposing accidentals. Let's see what we get this way."

Dax waited while Marlow's fingers danced over the computer keys. Columns of numbers and symbols flowed over the screen. After a while she said, "Get anything?"

Marlow said, "Nothing is working as it's supposed to. I think we're going to have to try the Chaos Machine."

"What's that?" Dax asks.

"It's paradox personified. We have a saying: 'There's nothing chaotic about the Chaos Machine. It just seems so at first.'"

"Why all this equipment?" Dax asked, soon after they had the project under way. "I can understand the computers. But what does a mathematician need or want with electrical apparatuses, alembics, retorts, furnaces, vats, chemicals?"

"I'm not just a mathematician," Marlow said. "I am a physical mathematician with alchemical leanings. Do you think that only chemists find uses for retorts and test tubes, and only physicists need electrical equipment? When you expect mathematics to change the world, you must give it an objective correlative. That's what your ancient alchemists, and ours, set out to do."

"But that stuff isn't needed any longer," Dax said.

"Are you so sure? We're in a difficult situation here. We need to make an impression on the nature of Nature itself. Mere talk won't suffice. We have to make our impression with physical means."

"I think I see what you're talking about," Dax said. "Just writing down a formula will not suffice. Not to bring about real change. Somehow that formula must be made objective, must be worked."

"That's right. The formula for a spaceship drive may work in theory. But that won't put it into practice. It must be actualized in a working model. Only then can we say that the universe is impressed by what we are doing, only then does the universe accept what we have done as one of the working rules."

"But how are we to build this objective correlative of how the universe ought to work?"

"I'll admit, that's the difficult part," Marlow said. "We must use our instincts. If we are far enough advanced in ourselves, we will build the correct model, and the universe will take heed. It will at the very least give us a clue."

Working together in a state of harmony, they built a machine more or less by instinct. Dax's tidy mind balked at this way of doing it, but doing things by how they felt seemed to be how science worked on Laertes. Neither of them could say why they put a condenser here and a reaction coil there. Something seemed to guide them. It was a knowledge that what they were doing was *possible*. That this was the way, the only way at this present moment in the ongoing history of space-time, the only way to get the result they needed.

And the machine grew. It looked like an assemblage or a caricature of some inconceivable machine. It had fenders, generators, governors, coils, springs, headlights, and things that seemed to have grown of their own accord, strangely formed parts to perform incomprehensible functions. When power was applied, the machine moved, though it would be more correct to say that it jittered and danced. Yet it didn't seem to *do* anything.

"That's to be expected," Marlow said. "It isn't finished yet."

"How will we know when it's finished?"

"It'll start doing what it's supposed to do. That's always the proof positive, when the form you invent produces the function you desire."

"And how long will that take?"

Marlow shrugged. "How should I know? Another ten minutes? Or two more lifetimes? I can't say."

"But that's irrational!"

"Anomalies are also irrational," Marlow reminded her. "Complexity Theory, at its very core, is irrational. We have to use the irrational to return to the rational."

"If you say so," Dax said. She wasn't entirely convinced by Marlow's line of reasoning. But she had no better suggestion herself. And the sheer weirdness of it began to appeal to her.

They labored on. The machine grew, spread, acquired more complexity. It did all sorts of things when you started it up. Wheels turned and balance-beams tilted. Gears changed the ratios of drive wheels, and the drive wheels were engraved with symbols that Marlow claimed had great intrinsic power.

And as the machine grew larger and more complex, it soaked up energy. The lights in the lab started to flicker and go out. More power was needed. Marlow made an emergency phone call and talked the city into putting in another high-power line.

"I don't understand where all the power is going," Dax said.

"Never mind. It's a good sign," Marlow said. "If there are unexplained discrepancies in energy, that's evidence we're on the right track."

"But what result are we trying for?"

"We'll know it when it happens," Marlow said. "Now let's get back to work."

The hours blended into one interminable hour that seemed to run forever. Dax called on all her reserves of energy and determination. She wondered how Marlow, with his frail frame, was able to continue at this pace. Even her healthy body was starting to feel the wear and tear of so long a time of working, thinking, doing. And the machine continued to grow.

They became a little drunk with their enterprise. Marlow insisted that they'd work better that way, that fatigue was a better friend to a creative scientist than a careful schedule of what to do next. The fatigue was like a drug, and Dax began to find it intoxicating. She moved like a sleepwalker, and yet her movements were precise in a somnambulistic way. They ordered in more and more equipment, and their suppliers, catching the fever, delivered the stuff to them at express speeds. And soon they had filled the entire great room with the machine, and Marlow had to continue the machine in an adjoining room, which soon became clogged with power cables and accumulators.

When they were finished, the Chaos Machine stood about eight feet high. A mass of parts, some of metal, some of glass or crystal, wired together in rough and ready fashion. Like a surrealistic view of mechanics. Dax could hear some sort of a motor in it just turning over, tick, tick, tick, a faintly ominous sound, as of something not right that nevertheless had come into existence. Light glinted off the machine's surfaces. A whiff of ozone, and something else Dax couldn't immediately identify. She thought it was like the smell of some rough beast.

Side-lit, the machine threw a monstrous shadow, seemingly not of itself, the shadow of something that did not exist, could not exist, but existed nonetheless. It was blocky and square at some angles, at others curved and fantastical, and at still others nip-waisted with great bulges above and below, like a creature that was struggling to free itself from the machine that had unaccountably given it birth.

At last Marlow decided it was as close to done as it would ever get.

"Now what?" Dax asked.

"Okay," Marlow said, "now we got to feed the problem into it."

"How?" Dax wanted to know.

Marlow shrugged. "Unfortunately, what we want to do is not literally possible. We can't tell it the real problem. So we'll put in the first approximation and hope for the best."

"Why can't you feed in the real problem?" Dax asked.

"Because there's no way of stating it precisely. And the machine would twist its meaning anyway. That's why we go with the first approximation."

"And if the first approximation is wrong?" Dax asked.

"So much the better," Marlow said.

When Marlow fed the problem in there was a great flashing of lights and a squeal of metal surfaces. The machine started shaking and trembling. An odd noise came from it.

"What is that sound?" Dax asked.

Marlow listened for a while, then said, "It's an old melody. 'Jeannie with the Light Brown Hair,' according to the readout."

"How does it pick up a song from Earth?" Dax asked.

"If we knew that, we'd really be getting somewhere," Marlow said. "Here comes the message."

On the Chaos Machine, the glittering surfaces vibrated and rippled, and then were still. On a monitor, a readout appeared.

"What does it say?" Dax asked.

Marlow read it aloud. "'You are about to lose Eridani 7 unless you cancel immediately.'"

"How did it do that?" Dax asked.

"If we knew that, we'd really be getting somewhere."

"Look," said Dax. "There's something else."

Marlow read, "'This is an unauthorized communication. You have been warned.'"

"What's Eridani 7?" Dax asked.

"That's one of the more important stars in our local federation! We don't want to lose that one!" He hastily adjusted the controls. The Chaos Machine gave a loud high-pitched whine and then settled down.

"That's better," Marlow said.

"What's it doing now?" Dax asked.

"It's signaling that something has come into its reception chamber."

"You never said anything to me about a reception chamber," Dax said.

"I never provided for one. The machine must have created it. Let's see where it put it."

They searched the lab, and in a corner found a closet with the door closed, from which a thin green gas seeped.

"Do you think that's it?" Dax asked.

"I don't see what else it could be. Let's open it and see what we've got."

Marlow unlocked the door and opened it. Within, sitting on a pile of freshly laundered shirts, was a small humanoid who looked up and blinked in the harsh light.

"And who are you?" Marlow asked.

But Dax knew at once. "Changu!" she exclaimed.

"I beg your pardon?" said Marlow. "I am not familiar with that word."

"It is a name rather than a word," Dax said. "This is my old teacher of hyperspatial mathematics, Changu. It's been years—centuries, in fact, since I've seen him. How are you, Changu?"

"I was a lot better before this interference in my affairs." Changu was indignant at being snatched from his comfortable underground classroom on a planet near Bootes.

"I'm sorry," Dax said. "I had no idea the Chaos Machine would pick you up like this."

"You might have foreseen it," Changu said. "What else would you expect of a Chaos Machine? Especially when it doesn't have a Two Max Comptroller."

"We still haven't developed that," Marlow said.

"You will," Changu said. "In a couple of years."

"Could you give me a clue?" Marlow said. "So I could get started on it?"

"Sorry, that's not allowed." Changu turned to Dax. "Dax, I do have something that will interest you. I've brought along the latest copy of recent discoveries in Vulcan tenth-order derivatives. I've got a copy of it right here."

Marlow couldn't care less about derivatives. Dax was delighted to see her old teacher again, and was interested in the latest research on Vulcan derivatives. Dax and Changu talked about Vulcan derivatives, searching for a way to apply them to the current problem.

They talked for a long time. Toward the end, Changu seemed to be scolding Dax. Then, abruptly, he disappeared.

"What was that all about?" Marlow asked.

"Changu was dressing me down for calling on him to help solve a problem I should be able to handle myself. Then he gave me a clue, and disappeared."

"What was the clue?" Marlow asked.

Dax said, "All he said was 'Ken is the answer.'"

'But what does it mean?'

"Seems pretty straightforward to me," Dax said. "We must find a Laertian named Ken. And we need to remember that what the phrase really means is, love is the answer."

"That's great," Marlow said. "Ken is a very common name among the Kendos. How are going to find this person in a population of millions?"

"I don't know," Dax said.

"Well, I have an idea about that," Marlow said. "You are going to have to see the Director. He's the only one who knows all the Kens and is empowered to give out Ken's address."

"I don't know where Kira is," Dax said. "I'll go myself."

Marlow nodded, but he was worried. It seemed to him that Complexity Theory and the Lampusan People's Party didn't let themselves be taken quite so lightly.

CHAPTER
63

DAX HEARD a loud and unfamiliar sound from outside Marlow's laboratory. "What's that?" she asked.

Marlow, standing near the window, glanced out, groaned, and said, "Oh, isn't that just what we needed."

Dax came to the window. Outside and below them she saw a crowd. There were some hundreds of individuals, men and women whose broad unthinking faces revealed them as Lampusans of the lowest class. They were shouting, waving their fists, and flourishing signs which read, FEDERATION GET OUT! NO ALIENS ON OUR PLANET! LEAVE OUR COMPLEXITY THEORY ALONE! LAMPUSAN VICTORY FOREVER! And other slogans of similar and unmistakable meaning.

"Where did they come from?" Dax asked.

"I see the hand of the Lampusan People's Party in this," Marlow said. "They undoubtedly hired these people and sent them here to harass us. They'll do anything to make their illicit theory work and win the election."

"Those people look pretty angry," Dax said.

Marlow nodded. "You can drive a Lampusan to homicidal frenzy if you pay him enough. That seems to be the case here."

"You wouldn't happen to have a back way out, would you?" Dax asked.

"As a matter of fact I do. But I greatly fear . . ."

Marlow led the way through rooms and corridors to the back of the house. It took no more than the least part of a glance to show that this exit was covered, too, by a smaller crowd than that in front, but an armed and angry crowd all the same.

When they heard a loud thumping noise from the front of the house, they hurried back to see what was happening. The Lampusans had plucked a comm tower from out of the ground and were using it as a battering ram, a dozen of them on either side of it, heaving it with a deadly rhythm against the door, which was already beginning to creak.

"This ceases to be amusing," Marlow said. "We could very well get ourselves killed while they continue these shenanigans. I suggest we swallow our pride and call for help."

Dax nodded and crossed quickly to a communicator on a pedestal stand. She picked it up, tapped it, grimaced, and replaced it.

"It's dead." She thought for a moment. "That comm tower . . ."

"They probably didn't even think of that themselves," Marlow said. "They just saw a handy piece of wood."

"Perhaps they were guided by synchronicity," Dax suggested. "Or do I mean serendipity?"

"You mean Complexity Theory," Marlow said. "It's showing its damnable hand again. You know, this would be a convenient time for your friend Major Kira to put in an appearance."

They could hear the door beginning to come apart under the repeated blows of the pole.

"But under the circumstances," Marlow said, "I think we're going to have to fend for ourselves. Pity I never keep any weapons here. They'd come in handy just about now."

"What about the Chaos Machine?" Dax asked. "Is there some way we could use it?"

"We just have used it. It has solved our problem. Ken is the answer, remember?"

"Of course I remember," Dax said. "But I'm talking about our current problem." She gestured at the door.

"It's out of the question," Marlow said. "The Chaos Machine deals with mathematics, not with angry people."

"Well, they're numbers, too," Dax pointed out.

Marlow paused to consider. "Yes, I suppose you're right. I suppose they are. Let me think for a moment."

"Don't take too long," Dax said.

"I've got it now. Chaos Machine! Can you hear me?"

"Of course I can," the Chaos Machine said. "I may be mathematical but I'm not deaf."

"Could you do something about those people breaking down the door?"

"What do you expect me to do? Lecture them? I'm not built for Exhortation, you know."

Dax said to it, "There are entities outside the door."

"Entities I understand," the Chaos Machine said. "But could you define door for me?"

"Consider it a membrane," Dax said. "A membrane under stress."

"Got it," said the Chaos Machine.

"Well, then. About those entities on one side of the membrane. Would you mind subtracting them from the situation?"

"I can't subtract all of them. That's not allowed. You have to leave one."

"All right. Leave one. A small one."

"And what should I do with the ones I subtract?"

"Store them somewhere in digital form," Dax said. "We'll want to put them back later."

"Got it," the Chaos Machine said, and went into its weird electromechanical dance. It shook and jiggled and bounced and clattered and timpanied and rang and dazzled, and soon a great cry came up from the people in front of the house, and then there was silence, and after that a single thin wailing voice.

Going to the window, Dax saw that the crowd that had been wielding the comm tower had disappeared. Only one man was left, and he was undersize. The rest of the crowd had backed away to a respectable distance.

"Great!" said Dax. "Now subtract all the rest. Except one, of course."

"I'm terribly sorry," the Chaos Machine said, "but I can't do that."

"Why can't you?"

"Because they're not doing anything. I'm not programmed to perform operations on entities not in motion."

"They're moving around and shuffling their feet," Dax pointed out.

"Yes. But that must be considered revolving in place, and does not affect the fact that they are technically at a state of rest."

"That's a pretty silly machine," Dax said.

"It follows its own logic," Marlow said, somewhat stiffly. "And anyhow, it saved our lives."

"But we're still trapped in here," Dax pointed out.

"Now," Marlow said, "would be a very convenient time for your Major Kira—"

Just at that moment the communicator on Dax's chest emitted a chirping sound.

Dax slapped it. "Yes?"

"Kira to Dax. How are things going there?"

"Listen up," Dax said. "I've got quite a few things to tell you."

236

KIRA TURNED OFF the communicator and looked around. Her first thought was to go to the aid of her colleague. But Dax had told her not to do that. Dax had the situation well in hand. Even though the Chaos Machine wouldn't do anything to get them out, apparently it could be relied upon not to let anyone in. Dax had urged Kira to go to the Director of Kendo Studies in downtown Sgheel. According to Marlow, he was the one man who could be counted on to know which was the correct Kendo, the one referred to by old Changu. Accordingly, Kira caught a public car and asked to be taken to the Metropolitan Statistics Building, where Marlow had thought the Director was most likely to be found.

The Metropolitan was a huge marble building with intricate sculptures around the pediment and tablature.

Kira found a clerk who didn't seem to have much to do and said, "I'd like to see the Director."

The clerk gave her a strange look. "Whom do you represent?"

"I am an officer of the *Deep Space Nine* space station."

The clerk had already taken in her uniform, but seemed unconvinced. "Do you have any identification?"

Kira showed her combadge.

"But how do I know you didn't steal that from the real Major Kira? I'm not making any accusations, you understand. Just trying to cover all possibilities." Kira glared dangerously at him.

"I guess you're all right," he said, backing down.

"I should think so!" Kira said. "And now will you please tell me where to find the Director? This is an urgent matter."

"I'd really like to oblige," said the clerk. "But it isn't quite so simple. He might be in several different locations within this building."

"Can't you call?"

"The Director never answers his communications."

"Well, tell me where you think he might be and I'll look for myself."

The clerk described three locations, each a considerable distance from the others, but all within the building.

"Thank you," Kira said. She turned to go, then asked, "Why doesn't he answer his communications?"

"Obviously, he doesn't want anyone to know where he is."

"But why doesn't he?"

The clerk looked around, saw no one within earshot, and said, "He's afraid of assassins."

Kira wanted to know more, but the clerk decided he had said too much as it was. "Oh, there's my communicator," he said, though Kira didn't hear anything. He hurried away to a back office. Kira shrugged and began her exploration.

At first it seemed straightforward enough. Her first stop was Floor 3, Room 100B. She took a turbolift and punched the button for the third floor. But when the door opened, she found she was on the fifth. A sign on the wall read, FLOOR 3 HAS BEEN TEMPORARILY REDESIGNATED FLOOR 6A.

She returned to the elevator, found a button for 6A, pressed it. The elevator took her to Floor 6, and announced that only the B-rank elevators went to Floor 6A. She returned to the ground floor, found the B-rank elevators, and started again.

After many complications she reached 6A, and walked down a corridor that should have led her to Room 100B. All of the rooms on that floor seemed to be in the 500 series. A sign on the wall said that all rooms were being temporarily reassigned, and that to reach room 100B she should proceed to the T (for temporary) series 800 series on Level JJ.

It seemed clear to her that the numbering of floors, levels, and rooms was purposely complicated, determinedly irrational. She found a padd in her shoulder bag. As she walked, she took notes on numbering and nomenclature. It seemed the only way of making any sense at all of the building.

She passed guards with drawn weapons, looking all around, but apparently not too sure what they were looking for. In any event, they made no attempt to stop her.

Kira hurried on her way, imbued with a strong sense of urgency. She thought of Dax, beleaguered in Marlow's laboratory. She thought of Commander Sisko trying to prevent the final sell-off of the station and its equipment. She even had a thought for Quark, caught in a losing game that had been initiated by his own greed. And here she was, going up ramps and down corridors, passing doors numbered in maddening nonsequentiality, losing time trying to find a Director who quite evidently didn't want to be found. And all the time she methodically checked out her findings on the padd.

This careful approach finally netted results. When she got back to Floor 6, Level 2, and started down the corridor, she saw that she was among the 200-series rooms. But hadn't they been the 400 series just a few minutes ago?

Senses alerted, she turned around, hurried down the corridor the way she had just come, turned a corner, turned another corner, and came upon a man in the act of changing the room numbers.

The man saw her and tried to run. Kira collared him before he got more than a few steps away.

He was a slender young man, and he had a nervous, harassed look.

"What is the meaning of this?" Kira demanded. "You're doing this on purpose, aren't you? Changing the room numbers to keep me confused."

"There's nothing personal about it," the man said. "I'm supposed to keep everyone confused. It's just until after the election."

"What happens then?"

"We go back to a rational system after the danger of assassination to the Director is passed. Now, if you will kindly let me go . . ."

Kira tightened her grip on the man. "I am an officer from DS9. Do you know what that is?"

"Of course," the man said. "You people are our only hope, now that Complexity Theory is running against us."

"We can't do a thing unless you help us," Kira said. "I need to find the Director."

"But he left orders that he's not to be found. It's because—"

"Of assassins, I know. But I'm not an assassin, and if I can't find him, I can't help him."

The man thought for a moment. "I guess there's something in that."

"Then will you help me find him?"

"Me? But I'm not authorized!"

"Then you'd better authorize yourself. If I don't find him, it's going to be Lampusans all the way."

The man thought for a long time. His face showed the agonizing indecision he was undergoing. At last he said, "I don't know exactly where the Director is. But I can take you to someone who does."

It was better than nothing. "Lead on!" Kira said.

The passage through the Statistics Building went a lot faster with the clerk leading the way. There was a whole system of back turbolifts that were hidden behind doors marked NO ADMITTANCE—STAY OUT—THIS MEANS YOU. Using them, they quickly arrived at a door marked CLOSED FOR REPAIRS. The clerk knocked. A woman's voice said, "Yes, what is it?"

The clerk opened the door and led Kira into a well-furnished office. At a large desk sat a large woman in a no-nonsense hairdo, with a severe expression on her face.

The clerk said, "Allow me to present an officer from *Deep Space Nine*. She urgently needs to see the Director."

"Does she?" the woman said in an ungracious tone. "A lot of people want to see the Director. Most of them are carrying weapons."

"Are we going to go through this again?" Kira asked.

"I suppose not," the woman said. "If you're an assassin, it's my husband's lookout, not mine." She turned to the back of the room, and, raising her voice, said, "Hey, Phrew! Somebody to see you!"

A door in the back of the room opened. A large ruddy-faced man peered out. "But I left express orders—"

"I have an urgent matter to take up with you," Kira said. "Your entire political system may depend on whether or not you can help me."

"Well, in that case," the Director said, "I guess you'd better come in."

In her usual crisp style, Kira got the formalities out of the way. "I'm looking for a Kendo named Ken. The message we got about him was 'Ken is the answer.' We think our informant must have been referring to a specific individual. You, it seems, are the only person who can help us find him."

"Ken is a very common name among us," the Director said. "I think I have an idea of whom your informant was referring to. Unfortunately, I can't tell you anything about him."

"Why not?"

"I'm in constant danger from the Lampusans," the Director explained. "But by being extremely cautious, I can hope to get through this election period alive. But if the Lampusans should win, and find out that I gave you special information that was to act against their election, my life here wouldn't be worth a plugged gold bar after they came into power."

"If you give me the information," Kira said, "you can prevent them from coming into power."

"I know. But the risk, if you should fail . . ."

"We are not going to fail!" Kira said.

"Perhaps not. But I can't be sure of that. And in the

absense of any other inducement . . . well, you can see my position."

"What would serve as an inducement for you?" Kira said.

The Director looked coy and didn't answer.

Kira decided to take the plunge. "How would you like to be president of Laertes after the Kendos win?"

"Now, that is a prize worth having," the Director said. "And worth taking some risks for. But are you sure you can swing it?"

"I'm sure," Kira said, remembering what Alleuvial had told her. He had offered the presidency to her. He could be relied upon to give it to her nominee. "Now, what about this person called Ken?"

"There's only one man in all Laertes your informant could have been referring to," the Director said. "He's the foremost dancing sculptor in all Sgheel. I'll write down his address for you. But don't tell anyone where you got it from—until after we win the election."

CHAPTER 65

Kira caught a public car to the downtown Artists' Quarter. Here the buildings were old and crowded close together. There were many theaters in this district, and a big collection of eating places. The tail end of a parade came through as she arrived, a parade complete with a brass band. There were little winding streets, cafes, and a man in a brown slouch hat who looked like a gypsy, cranking a barrel organ, with a monkey on a leash, a monkey with a little pillbox hat tied under his chin. Kira had never seen anything like him.

Kira wasn't sure she had come to the right place. She asked the gypsy, "Where am I?"

The gypsy said, "You're in the Artists' Quarter. This is where the artists live."

Kira already knew that upon their graduation from the University of Creative Arts, the government granted qualified artists a special dispensation. It included a living wage, and a special allowance for indulgences such as wine, women, song, and other matters artists find inspirational. They got free housing here in the Artists' Quarter. To live here had become de rigueur for scribblers and daubers from all over the Gamma Quadrant.

Kira said, "I'm looking for the studio of an artist named Ken."

"Talk to the monkey," the gypsy said. "He knows all about it."

Feeling very, very foolish, Kira bent over and said to the monkey, "Hello there, can you help me find someone?"

"Why not?" said the monkey. "I am a fully accredited travel guide and sightseeing spielbarker. But first you must cross my palm with silver."

"I thought only fortune-tellers said that."

"I am a fortune-telling monkey."

Kira fished in her bag and found a silver Lampusan ten-dinar coin. She gave it to the monkey. He bit it, spit on it and wiped it, rubbed it, held it up to reflect sunlight. Finally he was satisfied and put it away in a little beaded purse he wore around his neck.

"Who are you looking for?"

"An artist named Ken."

The monkey scratched his head. "Are you by any chance referring to the famous Ken the Dancing Sculptor?"

"That's the one," Kira said.

"Oh, no," the monkey said. "This is really too easy. Can't you ask me a harder one?"

"I'm afraid not," Kira said. "That's what I need to know. I've got the address, but the street signs here are confusing."

"See this brick building just up the street? The one with the balustrades and the flying buttresses?"

"Hard to miss it," Kira said.

"That's his atelier, and the master himself is inside, composing. Don't disturb him if it isn't something important."

"It has to do with the fate of the galaxy," Kira said.

"That ought to catch his attention," the monkey said. "Though you can never tell with artists."

Kira thanked the monkey and the gypsy and crossed the street and went up the granite stairs of the big old brick building with the flying buttresses.

Inside she found herself in a big domed space. There was a double staircase going up to the upper floors. She could hear the sound of music wafting down from the upper regions. A small orchestra seemed to be playing ballet music. Kira went up, and found herself in a long hallway illuminated by a row of chandeliers. The music seemed to come from the end of the hall. Kira walked down, following the music, and she came to a room at the end of the hall. Entering, she beheld a sight the likes of which she had never seen before.

To one side was a small orchestra, its members formally dressed in black suits. In the center of the room, which had a polished ballroom floor, a man, dressed only in the lightest of gossamers, was dancing around an object that Kira couldn't make out at first.

Coming closer, she saw that it was a half-finished sculpture, standing on a raised plinth, an object about eight feet high, with the armature still sticking out of its top. On tables surrounding the armature were buckets, and these contained wet clay of various colors and consistencies. The artist was dancing now, beginning with a measured tread, and as he passed up and down the floor, he selected handfuls or scoops of clay and threw them at the armature. The orchestra picked up the tempo and the artist began dancing more and more wildly, performing a three-dimensional treatment of a Jackson Pollock method, not that Kira knew who Jackson Pollock was. The artist danced and capered, and the orchestra speeded up to keep up with him, and somewhere a great kettledrum was pounding, and the artist's steps were lighter, faster, clay flew in the air in multicolor globs, and settled miraculously on the armature. The accidental effects had a grace and artistry that it was difficult to imagine happening in any other way. The orchestra worked itself up to a frenzy, and then a climax, the dancer's feet flew, his feet, tap-equipped, beat out a frenzied rhythm on the polished ballroom floor, and with a final twirl the dancer threw on the last glob of clay, backed off to admire the effect, twirled again, and collapsed to the floor in a grateful curtsy.

Ken disappeared backstage, calling out, "I'll be right back." He vanished into a room in the rear. Kira heard the muffled sound of water running, and after a while Ken came back, dressed in a white bathrobe, his hair wet from his recent shower.

"Yes, what can I do for you? Which aspect of the media do you represent? I'd guess literary, if it weren't for your costume, which is more than a little unusual."

"I'm not media at all," Kira said.

"You're not? But the *Laertian Sun* said they were going to send reporters to cover the composition of my latest sculpture. Luckily I've caught the whole thing on the hidden recorders." He gestured at a bank of glassy eyes set high in the ceiling. Kira hadn't noticed them before. "The media always follow my work. I wonder what could have happened to them."

"There have been anomalies of various sorts recently," Kira said. "Maybe the press was caught up in one. Have you heard about those?"

"I don't think I have," Ken said, frowning with effort as he tried to remember. "I don't stay up on politics or science or current events. I don't suppose these anomalies you speak of have much significance on the art scene, do they?"

"Perhaps not," Kira said. "Except in the sense that if they continue, all civilization might perish, and that would include all art."

"That wouldn't be so good," Ken said. "Planetary civilizations rise and fall, but art goes on forever. Though now that you mention it, it's a little difficult to see how art would continue if there were no artists or audience left."

"It would be a problem," Kira said. "It's that very problem I'm here to make sure won't happen."

"Well, that's a good thing," Ken said. "Have you traced one of those anomalies here, to my studio? How exciting! I'd love to sculpt an anomaly."

"That's not exactly what I had in mind," Kira said. "I need your help. I don't suppose you've ever heard of a woman named Allura, who is gambling at present on DS9?"

"I think I've heard of DS9," Ken said. "Artificial satellite, is it?"

"Not exactly. It's a space station."

"Oh, well, comes to much of the same thing. Well, what about this station?"

"A Lampusan woman named Allura has come there and is gambling. She is winning past all possibility of such an event happening. She is winning the entire station. But that is not the only difficulty. Her winning has been accompanied by a series of increasingly dire scenarios, anomalies, as we call them, which are threatening all civilization. It's all tied to Allura. It is necessary to stop this woman somehow."

"Yes, quite," Ken said. "But why have you come to me? And anyhow, if she is as you say a Lampusan woman, she can be counted on to stop herself. That's one of the things the Lampusans excel at. We call it shooting off your foot to remove your shoes. Give a Lampusan a little power, he always goes too far and ends up losing everything."

"So I've heard. But it looks like this time might be different. If Allura continues to win at DS9, it seems certain that her party, the Lampusan People's Party, will win the upcoming planetwide election here on Laertes."

"Indeed?" said Ken. "That would be bad! Kendos frighten their children with tales of how bad it would be if the Lampusans came to power. But it can't be! That would be contrary to the way of nature which has decreed that Lampusans be eternal underdogs!"

"But that is what is happening."

Ken thought about it. He looked distraught, distracted. Finally he said, "Assuming what you tell me is true—it would waste far too much time if I assumed otherwise—then what could you possibly want me to do?"

"I don't know, exactly," Kira said. "But your name was put forward as the only one that could make a difference."

"But what do you *want* of me?"

"I want you to come with me to DS9," Kira said. "You're our only hope at this point. I don't know exactly what I want of you. I just know that you've been pointed out as one who could make a difference."

"You know," Ken said, "I've always believed that about myself. That I was one who could make a difference."

"Then come with me!"

"But I'll miss my work schedule!"

"Bring your sketch pad," Kira said. "Maybe you'll get inspiration from the new surroundings."

"Yes, I could do that," Ken said. "And I could bring some modeling clays, just in case I see some shapes that inspire me."

"That's the idea!" Kira said.

"All right!" said Ken. "I'll be ready in ten minutes. Would you mind if we take my ship?"

"Not at all," Kira said. "As it happens, we're in need of transport."

CHAPTER
66

BASHIR DIDN'T LIKE the way Allura turned to gelatin as soon as she heard that Kira and Dax were returning to the ship with a visitor from Laertes, someone with the reputation of being a famous artist.

"What's his name?" Allura demanded.

"It's something simple," Bashir said, "like Steve or Dan or Ron. But it's slipped right out of my mind."

"Is it Ed?"

"No, that's not it."

"Tom?"

"Not that, either."

"Can't you find out?"

"I suppose I could ask Commander Sisko," Bashir said. "But he'll think it's odd."

"Ask him! Please! Please!"

"Oh, all right," Bashir said. He was annoyed at her. But she was really very pretty. And terminally desirable. Not that that was helping him any. He knew she was bad news. Still, when he looked at her, his brains seemed to turn into mush. He knew that this thing couldn't go on. This mad passion of his, as he considered it—or petty infatuation combined with childish stubbornness, as Odo diagnosed it—was leading him and his friends to ruin.

His combadge chirped. "Commander?"

"Yes, Julian."

"That new fellow who's arrived from Laertes."

"What about him?"

"Is his health okay? I just thought as doctor I ought to ask."

"He's doing fine."

"Thanks, Commander."

"If there isn't anything else, I have some work to do."

"Certainly. Oh, Commander! By the way—what was his name?"

"Ken," Sisko said.

"First name or last?"

"Just the one, as far as I could make out."

"Thanks. I just wondered. And you said he's an artist of some sort?"

"Yes. A dancing sculptor, whatever that is."

"It does sound strange. Okay, thanks, Commander."

Hanging up, Bashir told Allura what he had learned.

"Ken!" she breathed. "The famous dancing sculptor!"

"I didn't know he was famous," Bashir said.

"On Laertes he's very famous."

"I don't see why it makes any difference," Bashir said.

"I wouldn't expect you to," Allura said.

"What's that supposed to mean?"

"Never mind. Time you went to the gambling tables. Do you think Quark would let me in?"

"I suppose I could ask him," Bashir said.

"No, I'll go down with you and we'll ask him together. I simply must see this Ken."

"Well, let's go," Bashir said ungraciously, and walked out of the suite without even waiting for Allura to follow him. He was feeling really lousy. Funny the way a beautiful woman could do that to you.

CHAPTER 67

"FINE STATION you've got here, Commander," Ken said.

"Thanks," Sisko said. "I used to like it a lot, back when it was mine."

"I've heard you've had a run of bad luck," Ken said. They were walking down the Promenade toward Quark's Place. Dax and Kira, just returned from Laertes, were walking a few steps behind. Not because they felt inferior. They didn't. But in order to give Sisko and Ken a chance to get acquainted.

"I've heard about your bad luck," Ken said. "That's why I'm here. That's what they told me."

"We're hoping for the best," Sisko said.

"But what do you expect me to do?" Ken asked.

"I'll be damned if I know," Sisko said. "I thought you'd have an idea."

"Not a clue, I'm afraid. Not that I don't want to help."

"Are you a skilled gambler, by any chance?" Sisko asked.

"Not at all. I'm a dancing sculptor, not a gambler."

Dax stepped in at this point, since Sisko was clearly growing exasperated. "It's probably best if we just put Ken into the situation and see what develops."

Sisko had to be content with that. He had been spending some unhappy time alone in his quarters. It wasn't really his any longer. Quark had lost it several hours ago. But the Gamemaster had been kind enough to let him use it "until we tie up the final odds and ends," as he put it. So Sisko had sat and thought. He never could have imagined he'd have gotten so fond of a place until now when he was on the verge of losing it. He didn't know what the Federation Council would do about this. There would have to be a general court-martial, of course. With a little luck he might come out of that all right. After all, it wasn't his fault the station was lost. Would they cite him for inactivity? But what could he have done?

These and many other gloomy thoughts rolled around in his head as he walked toward Quark's Place with Ken. This most recent turn of events didn't please him, either. How could a dancing sculptor help, even if he was a famous one?

LISETTE V.D. RIDDER
CORN. EVERTSENSTR 7
3572 JP UTRECHT
NETHERLANDS
(030) 715540

CHAPTER
68

THERE WAS A CROWD in Quark's Place. Quark had learned that even if he was losing at gambling, he could make pretty good side money by selling seats to the destruction of DS9. He had established a book on it, and stood to make a profit either way it went. It wouldn't take care of his really calamitous losses, in which he had lost not only all the proceeds of his gambling and other businesses, but also the station, to the Lampusan woman.

He was feeling good this evening. Commander Sisko had come up with an unexpected hundred thousand credits. That bought a little time.

"Tonight," he told Rom, "put away all the small glasses. All drinks tonight are to be large."

"Should we charge more?" Rom asked.

Quark smiled. What a question! "What do *you* think?" he asked.

"Yeah, I'd guess quite a lot more. Double?"

"Multiplied by ten is what I had in mind," Quark

said. "After all, this is likely to be the last night of the gambling. After tonight, I'm really, completely, and irrevocably tapped out."

"Won't the Gamemaster advance you any more credit?"

"He can't. An investigating commission from Laertes has just announced their imminent arrival. And anyhow, all I'm doing is losing. It's time, in the old proverb of the Ferengi people, to fold our tents like the Gortz and silently steal away."

The Gortz were a race that had stolen away so successfully that they had been missing for several centuries. The story was used whenever a Ferengi wanted to make a particularly dire point.

Rom said, "Brother, I think perhaps I can help."

Quark looked at him levelly. "I doubt that very much. But what did you have in mind."

"This." Rom took a thick envelope out of his pocket and handed it to Quark.

Quark opened it and took out a bundle of latinum strips. He thumbed through them quickly. They amounted to a respectable sum.

"Where did you get these?"

"Never mind, brother. You said you needed money to continue your gambling operation. I have brought you money."

"You do well to conceal your sources of credit," Quark said. "This is a useful amount, brother. It will help us extend our gambling a little longer. It may even turn the tide, who knows? And if not, we will go away."

"Where can we go after this?" Rom asked.

"Wherever games of chance are tolerated, a Ferengi can make his way. That means everywhere."

"Good to know that," Rom said.

"Here they come now," said Quark. "Remember about the glasses!"

Folded seats had been set up, and mirrors positioned so everyone could see the action. There were several hundred people crowded into the small room. Quark hurried over and shook Sisko's hand as he entered.

"So glad to see you here, Commander! And Dax and Kira, how nice! And this I imagine is your guest."

"I'm Ken," Ken said, shaking Quark's hand.

"Delighted," said Quark. "I've reserved seats for you all. Sorry it's so crowded. Everyone has been anxious to see this one. Ah, here comes Dr. Bashir, and if I'm not mistaken, that's Allura with him!"

Allura said, "I know you don't want me in here, Quark, but I thought that, given the circumstances, you might relent."

"And you thought right, my dear," Quark said. "It's just about all over now anyhow. You couldn't have done better if you'd been gambling yourself. In fact, perhaps you'd like to do it yourself, in these final sessions? You against me? What do you say?"

"I think I'd prefer Julian to continue, for the moment, anyhow," Allura said.

Bashir's face was tense as he made his first bet. Allura was beside him but she was staring at Ken. The dancing sculptor was watching the play intently, but a dispassionate observer would have to admit that he was aware that Allura was nearby. But not very aware. Ken was like a golden god. He glowed with Kendo high spirits. The dice rattled. The cards flashed. Numbers streaked across the screen. The toteboards whirled. And there was a result, and a sigh ran through the audience.

"Dead tie," Quark announced.

"Commander," Kira whispered, plucking at Sisko's sleeve.

"What is it?" Sisko said. "This is interesting, I want to watch this."

"Someone wants to see you urgently."

"Later."

"Sir, it's Captain Adams."

Sisko sighed loudly. "All right, I'm coming."

CHAPTER
69

"GOOD TO SEE YOU, Commander."

"And you, Captain."

"The reason I asked for you," Adams said, "is because we're positioned and ready and Starfleet has placed us under your command. We could take the Gamemaster's ship over in half an hour if you give the word. Then it wouldn't matter what their threats were."

There was a subtle disturbance. A shimmering in the air. It solidified, and there was a person there. Sisko's first impression was that it was a small person. Then, looking more carefully, he saw it was a child, a boy.

"And who are you?" Sisko asked.

"Wait a minute," Kira said. She had come along with Sisko. "I know you! You were working the computer in the Lampusan People's Party Headquarters."

"You got sharp eyes," the kid said. "I'm Timbo, and I'm here to tell you, hands off."

"I suppose you're going to stop us?" Sisko asked.

"No. But I can tell you here and now, you make a single move against the outcome of the theory and you're in trouble. The theory is in its fulminating stage now. It's gone through enough series of developments that it's become quasi-sentient. It has a desire now to see itself come to fruition without interference. I won't be responsible for what happens if you try to thwart that will."

"How do you know all this?" Kira asked.

"Because I am the Chief Mathematician for the Lampusan People's Party."

"This is crazy," Adams said. "Ben, are you going to let a child sway your judgment?"

"If so, it won't be for the first time," Sisko said, remembering other times, other decisions.

"What are you going to do?" Adams asked.

Sisko stood there, and words formed in his throat. Before he could speak, Dax came through the door, running.

"Benjamin! Something has happened!"

"What?" Sisko asked. "Come on, Dax, out with it!"

Dax said, "After the tie round, when you left, Quark called for a pause. And then he asked Ken if he'd like to take over the bank. Ken acted like it didn't matter much to him, but he said if Quark wanted him to, he'd be pleased to. When Allura heard that, she came forward and said, 'With this change in circumstances, I'd like to play Andralor directly against the great Ken!' Quark retired and the game started again, only this time it was Ken managing what was left of the ship's resources, and Allura playing with her own money that Bashir had won for her."

"Yes?" Sisko said. "And what happened?"

"Nothing yet."

"Let's check it out," Sisko said.

Gamble

WHEN SISKO, with Adams along, reached Quark's,
they saw Bashir, shoulders slumped, face drawn, a
picture of dejection, leaving the gambling position
and taking a seat in the audience. Allura walked past
him to the punter's slot. She didn't even look at him.

Allura had dressed with particular care that morning, after hearing about Ken's arrival. She wore a
shimmering iridescent gown that changed color as the
overhead lights played on it, turning now green, now a
warm and glittering peach. Her hair was done up in
an elaborate style of ringlets. Her posture was erect,
even haughty. She seemed not even to glance toward
her opponent, Ken, who was standing tall and mo-
tionless, his blond hair stiffly combed and sending off
lights of its own. The two of them were standing
within a railed circle. Surrounding them was the
audience: several hundred people, including most of
the DS9 personnel. But there were observers from
other planets there, too—Vulcans, supercilious

Regulans, and a few of the recent groups that had an associate membership with the Federation. There was a quiet clink of glasses and rattle of silverware as people ate their Gambling Special Dinner—which Quark had catered at great expense to those who ordered it. In fact, this evening was going to cost anybody who cared to attend a pretty penny. But no one cared, it was the event of the year, the final minutes of the final game of the Galactic Series of Gambling.

Olix, the Ferengi priest, had also shown up for this final showdown. He sat in a back row, his hands folded into deep sleeves, his expression impassive.

There were a lot of well-known people here. Word of this showdown had traveled across the galaxy at faster-than-light speeds. If Quark had had a few more weeks to advertise, he could have filled the Spiral Nebula, if it had been available for this purpose.

Quark, standing near the entrance, noted with satisfaction how the place was filling up. He was suffused with joy. Not only was he putting on an affair that was the envy of any Ferengi, he had also set it up so that the viewing profits were his entirely. It was true that he still owed a fortune on the station he had lost. But this little bonanza would at least give him maneuvering room. Life was not so bad after all!

Now, seeing that the moment was at hand, he stepped forward.

"Ken," he said, "I now entrust you with the proceeds of the station, and with the honor of gambling on behalf of DS9. Do you accept this high charge?"

"Indeed I do," Ken said. "Furthermore, I'm prepared to back this venture with my entire personal resources."

"I admire your spirit," Quark said. "Especially since one of the provisions of our contract, which in your haste you might not have read, gives the house, which is to say, me, fifty percent of your winnings, if any, and absolves the house entirely from your losses."

"If any," Ken put in.

"Yes, exactly," Quark said. "And now, if everyone is ready, let the gambling begin."

At Quark's signal, one of his Ferengi assistants threw an Andralor ball into the air. There was a hush as Ken made his first bet.

"What a paltry sum," Allura scoffed. "I'll see your bet and double it!"

Action from the outset! This was what the audience had paid plenty to see.

Ken smiled, a brief, dazzling smile, and pushed out his markers. The Andralor balls spun in the air . . .

Sisko couldn't bear to watch any more. He left and returned to his quarters.

CHAPTER 71

THERE WAS A TAP on the door of Sisko's office.

"Come in," Sisko said.

The door opened. Dax entered.

"Benjamin," she said, "what are you doing here? Why aren't you down at Quark's watching the action?"

"Frankly," Sisko said, "I'd rather not know what happens."

"I understand your feelings," Dax said.

She settled back into a comfortable chair. Sisko could hear a faint whispering sound in the quiet room.

"What's that?" he asked.

Dax said, "I'm following the action on my combadge. I had the computer patch me in."

"Oh . . ." Sisko fiddled with the baseball on his desk, then looked up as he heard a faint increase in the communicator's volume.

"What's that?"

"Oh, just an unusually big win," Dax said. "The audience is applauding."

"I see. Who won?"

"You don't really want to know, do you?" Dax said maliciously.

"Yes, I do! Tell me what happened."

"Ken redoubled Allura's last bet."

"Yes. And?"

"And won."

"He won? You're sure?"

"I'm quite sure. Just a minute, there's an announcement. . . . Yes, Ken has just won the power systems. And Benjamin, he has donated them to you!"

"You mean we've got the power systems back?"

"That's exactly what I mean," Dax said.

"I can't tell you how pleased I am," Sisko said. "I never thought I'd get sentimental about power systems! Wait until Chief O'Brien hears about this!"

"He must know," Dax said. "He's down at Quark's along with everyone else, watching it all happen. Wait a minute!"

Sisko waited. Finally he couldn't stand it any longer. "What's going on?"

"The players are making an intricate series of bets," Dax said. "They're doubling and redoubling each other like there's no tomorrow. Come to think of it, that might be the situation! Damn!"

"What's the matter?" Sisko said. "What's happening?"

"I've lost the link," Dax said, taking the communicator ear and first shaking it and then tapping it on the arm of her chair.

Sisko was on his feet. "Come on!" he said to Dax.

"But where are we going?" she asked innocently.

"To Quark's! I can't stand this any longer!"

CHAPTER
72

WHEN SISKO ENTERED Quark's, he was surprised by the sudden round of applause that greeted him. He looked around, sure it had to be for someone else. But there was no one near him except Dax, and she was clapping, too. Ben's first instinct was to get the hell out of there as quickly as he could. If there was one thing he was conscious of, it was his dignity. Now, with the applause ringing, his first thought was, Somebody's kidding; they're trying to put something over on me. It had to be some sort of a practical joke. Then Quark came over, grinning broadly, and Sisko's mind hardened. If that little Ferengi thought he was going to put anything over on Sisko, he'd better think twice!

But Quark was reaching out and shaking his hand. Adams was there, grinning. Others were coming around, too, slapping Sisko on the back, grinning, and Sisko let his guard relax enough to ask, "What's going on?"

"They're applauding you, Commander," Kira said, coming out of the crowd and taking his arm.

"But what for?"

"For standing firm the way you did. For not panicking and letting Starfleet take over. For having the faith that this thing could be solved without violence and bloodshed."

"I really didn't have much choice," Sisko said.

"You had every choice in the world," Kira said.

"But I don't understand what's happened," Sisko said. "The last thing I knew, Allura had the station."

"That's all over," Kira said. "Allura matched herself against Ken, and she lost."

Allura came forward then, with Ken. In fact it would have been difficult for her to move without him, because they had their arms around each other's waists.

Sisko could think of nothing more to say than, "So you lost finally, eh, Allura?"

"I wouldn't say that I lost as that Ken here won," Allura said. "There was something so masterful about his betting style . . . well, what could I do?"

"What indeed?" Sisko said. "You must be really pleased with yourself, Ken."

"Oh, yeah, I'm happy about the outcome," Ken said. "But what's most important to me is meeting this little lady here. She may be only a Lampusan, but she's everything to me." His arm tightened around Allura's waist. She simpered. He grinned. Sisko reminded himself not to throw up.

"You two had never met before?" Ben said conversationally.

"As a matter of fact, I'd never really met a Lampusan before," Ken said. "We Kendos sorta keep to ourselves. Tend to look down on the Lampusans, though I can't imagine why, to judge by this one here. She's really something special."

"Ken's going to teach me how to do dancing basketweaving," Allura said.

"She's got the perfect build for it," Ken said. "She'll be my protégée. And—may I say it?—my wife."

There was a general round of applause when he made the announcement. Sisko congratulated them both.

"What were the results of the election on Laertes?" Sisko asked.

"We lost, as usual," Allura said. But she didn't seem too cut up about it.

Just before they left, Sisko couldn't resist saying, "I guess your Lampusan People's Party will take it pretty hard, losing the election that way."

"I suppose so," Allura said. "But they're used to losing. But maybe that'll all start changing now. What do you think, Ken?"

"I wouldn't be surprised," Ken said. "If this isn't a win-win situation, I don't know what is."

And Sisko, thinking it over later, as he directed the work crews to get the place cleaned up, decided he wouldn't be surprised either.

CHAPTER
73

QUARK SAT in his back room, doing what a Ferengi loved best: counting money. There was plenty of it spread out on the table. It was in the form of gold-pressed latinum bars and a variety of alien currencies. His brother Rom sat in a corner, observing protocol by not getting within grabbing distance of his brother's heap. He was also performing his duty as a Ferengi younger brother: listening to Quark boast.

"Yes, I brought it off," Quark was saying, for perhaps the twentieth time in the last half hour. "Everyone thought it was impossible, but I showed them otherwise. Due to my perseverance and faith in the immutable odds, I broke that Lampusan woman and her Lampusan People's Party. I won back our station, and the money Sisko advanced me, and the money you advanced me too, Rom, most excellent younger brother! The station is back to where it was before all this began. And I am rich, Rom, rich! I won't bore you with numbers, but suffice it to say that

I've turned a very tidy profit indeed. And you share in my glory, of course."

"It is a most splendid result, brother," Rom said. "I give you innumerable congratulations. And I am so glad that I was able to be part of this triumph."

"I'm glad, too, Rom," Quark said. "You do deserve a little credit for raising that fifty thousand when things were tight. Who did you get it from? I'll repay them immediately."

"That would be good, brother," Rom said. "The money was advanced through the priest, Olix, and comes from the Charismatic Fathers of Profit and Loss."

"That's unusual," Quark said. "Our religious orders don't usually involve themselves in lay business."

"They did this time," Nog said. "With conditions, of course."

"I'd expect no less of them. What conditions?"

"Here is the agreement I signed in your name," Rom said, and handed Quark a legal document.

Quark scanned it. His smile turned into a frown. "Surely this is an error? This figure here?"

"No, brother. It is what I agreed to."

"But it says their investment is to receive two hundred percent interest. And the amount is to be compounded hourly until repayment!"

"I thought it was a little stiff, myself," Rom said. "But you said do what I had to do to raise it."

"You have ruined me! After paying this off—which I must do immediately in order to avoid further charges—I'm left with barely what I began with. Rom, they have cheated me!"

Rom hung his head. "I'm sorry . . . I thought you meant . . . I tried . . ."

Quark pulled himself together. He wasn't really

ruined. He had exaggerated in order to discomfit Rom. Actually, even with the exorbitant payment to the Charismatic Fathers, he had done very well. But there was no reason for Rom to know that. Such knowledge might give him a swelled head.

"You've done pretty well, considering," Quark said. "And if one must be bettered in a business deal, it is well that it happened at the hands of our own religious authorities rather than some stranger. Never a bad idea to be in good with religion! And what better way than by paying them a lot of money, eh?"

And so Quark went on counting his money content in the knowledge that once again he had done good by doing well. It was, after all, the fundamental lesson of his religion.

ACCEPTED AROUND THE COUNTRY, AROUND THE WORLD, AND AROUND THE GALAXY!

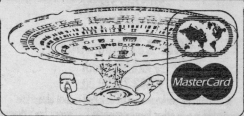

- No Annual Fee
- Low introductory APR for cash advances and balance transfers
- Free trial membership in The Official STAR TREK Fan Club upon card approval*
- Discounts on selected STAR TREK Merchandise

To apply for the STAR TREK MasterCard today, call

1-800-775-TREK

Transporter Code: SKYO

STAR TREK
THE NEXT GENERATION®

**Make it So: Leadership
for the *Next Generation*™**
by Wess Roberts, Ph.D., and Bill Ross
52097-0/$22.00
(available now)

Star Trek Blueprints
by Rich Sternbach
50093-7/$20.00
A beautifully packaged set of detailed actual blueprints
unavailable in any other form elsewhere — every fan's dream!
(Available mid-November 1995)

Crossover
A novel by Michael Jan Friedman
89677-6/$23.00
With Spock imprisoned in the Romulan Empire,
the generations must work together to prevent interstellar war.
(Available mid-November 1995)

POCKET
BOOKS